PURPLE AND FINE WOMEN

PURPLE AND FINE WOMEN

by

EDGAR SALTUS

With *an* Introduction *by*

W. L. GEORGE

1925
PASCAL COVICI *Publisher*
CHICAGO

AMS PRESS
NEW YORK

Reprinted from the 1925 edition
First AMS EDITION published 1968
Manufactured in the United States of America

AMS PRESS, INC.
New York, N.Y. 10003

Contents

Introduction

By W. L. GEORGE

IN his books the author places not only what he knows, but what he dreams; not only what he is, but what he would be. Half fact, half vision, thus is a book made. So when I take up a book that counts, by a man I never knew, I am curious not only of what he tells, but of what he is. Some authors, such as Flaubert, hide; others, like Mr George Moore, proclaim; yet others, and Saltus is one of these, peer at the reader like a nymph in the woods toying with a dull satyr, half-tempted to come out, yet instinctively reluctant. I do not suppose that many people understood Saltus; he had probably too much pride to expose himself easily. No doubt he shared with all of us the desire to express himself, but something held him back, that pride perhaps, a delicacy of feeling, a capacity for laughter which hides so much capacity for suffering. I feel all that as I read this book of stories. I am tempted to make a synthesis of what they reveal, to figure Saltus as he may have been.

Thus proceeding, I have a vision of an interesting,

erratic man, where dominate two characteristics: the first is Parisianism. France, the (reputed) Latins in general, convey to Saltus an idea of refinement, split ideas, delicate irony. His passion for France is shown by his continual use of French words and expressions, *à propos* of which it is worth saying that in no single instance does he make a mistake. This is a mere linguistic tribute, but it is worth paying since a reading of the most august English and American authors, even Henry James, occasionally yields absurdity in the use of French. Saltus, one feels, was permeated by France. It is said that an Englishman Italianate is a devil incarnate; upon an American the French influence is, as Mr Polly would have put it, more 'benifluous.' It gives to the American character a *je ne sais quoi,* a sort of icing akin to the gilded portion of the most luxurious type of cake. French influence suits America better than England; it sits upon the Englishman like pink ribbons on an elephant. The Englishman writing about the French is almost invariably imbecile. He sees them as picturesque, faintly pathetic and lightly humorous. Mr Leonard Merrick, whenever he writes about Tricotrin and his friends, exhibits the immense reservoir of ineptitude which lies behind the mind of a clever Englishman.

The American does not suffer so because the pink

ribbons sit better upon him; he wears them instead
of scarlet ribbons. He is not so afraid of giving himself away. Thus, in these stories, we find Saltus taking naturally to France, and particularly to the *grand
monde*. Saltus did not inherit from the nineties an
impulse to realism. He has no kinship with Zola,
whose soul, according to Mr Anatole France, was
too completely concerned with zinc factories and
flatirons. There are no flatirons in Saltus. He is
essentially oriental and fantastic. Drink is served in
a flask of gold. A party is given by the morganatic
widow of an emperor. He makes a world about him,
sensuous and æsthetic, a world of chinchilla, emer-
alds, and Malines lace, where evolve only people to
whom work is an incident, and perhaps love an ac-
cident. In this world he evolves as a philosophical
jester. He loves it, but he is not deceived by it, does
not take it seriously. In many of the stories he plays
a trick upon the reader. The conclusion is perhaps
not so much a trick as a revelation that the story is
not true. The reader has been taken in.

It may be that he describes himself on page one,
when he says: 'I had not a care on my mind, a regret on my conscience, a speck on my shoes.' One
conceives him again when he remarks: 'Frequentation with Epictetus makes one very civil.' I am sure
that Saltus was civil, providing one did not mind his

being a little *distrait*. One imagines him hating a
bore as Mrs F's aunt hated a fool. His mind is easily
wearied; in the middle of a story, his attention
wanders as he realizes with horror that the tale-teller
is about to become pathetic. He is essentially negli-
gent. Things are what they are, and things do happen: in the turmoil he sits, Olympian, but secretly
watchful of anything that might amuse him.

Through Saltus runs strongly the cynical strain.
When a lover relates his interview with the spirit of
his dead beloved, Saltus remarks: 'He grows lyri-
cal.' In the same story, he retorts to the haunted
lover that his shoemaker was annoyed by apparitions
of deceased customers. Of two lovers he observes
that 'they had interchanged all those lovely vows
which means so much and also so little.' He sums up
a vulgar rich woman who got into society by saying
that 'there was a sesame in her dollars.'

Thus Saltus, in the *grand monde*, remains unim-
pressed; he likes it as a show; he is never deceived
by it. When he introduces characters he is apt to call
them de Chose or de Machin. He does not give them
magnificent names. He ironically calls them 'Chose'
and 'Machin,' which is the French for Tom, Dick
and Harry. And no doubt he gives them a 'de' only
so that they may fit the atmosphere. To him they are
'de' because people are 'de,' and they are not de

much. One feels this again whenever the story drifts across a duke, for in the mind of Saltus the duke is always amiable, but wholly aimless. He is not on his knees to dukes, normal features of the landscape. They merely provide him with merriment. A continuous trickle of humor passes through his pages. The dowager in 'The Top of the Heap' is sister to the Oscar Wilde duchess. When Saltus causes the dowager to say of her son: 'He has a perfect mania for going to the dentist's, and that, I think shows so much conscientiousness,' we recognize that woman, and crave her acquaintance. Again, Saltus sums up a character as 'Alphabet Jones, a man of polite letters.'

Perhaps we strike the completely sincere Saltus whenever he talks about women. He has for them a perfectly French passion. He looks upon them, not only as utensils for reproduction, but angels fathered by demons; to an extent he agrees with Nietzsche in looking upon women as a reward, but he has a certain disdain for the warrior, and might say, parodying Nietzsche: 'Man is for art, and woman the reward of the artist.' Subject to an ironic outlook, Saltus loves women as they are, women as he sees them. He sees them in an atmosphere of light, color, scent, as exquisite phantoms which a kiss materializes. He speaks of 'the silk of her mouth.' A little further he gives an ideal description of his vision: 'Her eyes were pools of purple, her hair was a garland of flame,

her mouth a scarlet thread.' He himself applies the
mot juste to his own dream: Sultry. He defines
when he says: 'Her hair made a garland of gold.
Her eyes were sultry, her lips were scarlet.' In another story he rises further to definition: 'Her purple
eyes were sultry, her scarlet mouth was moist, the
red tangles of her hair made a burnous of flame, her
fingers glowed, and her wrists were such as those on
which, in days gone by, falcons alighted and kisses
fell.'

It is not easy to sum up Saltus, nor is it necessary.
I have lost the taste for classification, and I am not
concerned to know what place posterity will assign
to him. He may, in five hundred years, figure in the
cyclopedias of literature, or again he may not. If at
that time his tenuous spirit hovers in the Place Ven-
dome, or over the Corso, he may be moved by curiosity to note what they think of him after so long.
If anything is written there, he will probably laugh
at it, thinking it solemn and rather *pompier*. And if
nothing stands there, I am convinced that he will
truthfully remark: *'Je me'en fiche.'*

PURPLE AND FINE WOMEN

A Bouquet of Illusions

HAS THE FIGARO again succeeded in losing itself?

The temperature was heavenly. I had had a beautiful swim in the beautiful sea. I had breakfasted on dishes a poet had prepared. The evening previous I had passed with some of the most agreeable people in Europe. At baccarat, the night before, I had managed without effort to rid myself of ill-gotten gains. I had not a care on my mind, a regret on my conscience, a speck on my shoes. In spite of which, or perhaps precisely on that account, as I stood that morning in the reading-room of the Cercle de Biarritz I found nothing better to do than to affect annoyance because The Figaro was not under my monocle.

'Pardon, monsieur,' said the lackey to whom I had spoken. 'Behold a gentleman who is reading it.'

I had beheld the gentleman before. Who he was I did not know; but, to use a localism of the land, he had intrigued me. He had the appearance of a Somebody, the distinction that study and suffering bring.

He suggested perspectives and possibilities that the entirely amiable yet perfectly aimless dukes and princes by whom the club was frequented neglected to supply. Merely in the manner in which he turned his head there was manifest that preoccupation which is characteristic of those whose existence is cerebral. Twice already I had met him — once with one of the little Pignatelli princesses and once with the Prime Minister; but on each occasion his name had escaped me. Yet not the timbre of his voice. It was grave and deep, and presently in his beautiful baritone he addressed me, recalling an incident that had occurred at the Casino and asking whether I had won.

'Le baccarat apporte, emporte mais ne rapporte pas,' I answered, and after a few other platitudes I gathered up The Figaro, which meanwhile he had offered me. When I put it down he had gone.

On the morrow I met him on the road that skirts the Chambre d'Amour and which through kilometers of pines leads to the Adour, a river so beautiful in itself that all the ingenuity of Bayonne has been unable to make it wholly hideous. The next day I ran into him at Bidart, a hamlet so silent that you might fancy it enchanted by the spells and marvels of its languid afternoons. And again I encountered him on the Route d'Espagne, than which even the Corniche is not lovelier.

On these occasions we rode a while together, and
in the process I discovered that he was alarmingly
learned. He appeared to have been everywhere, met
everybody, and studied everything. He appeared,
too, to be remarkably intuitive, and flattered me —
very basely, I have since thought — by telling me I
was a born novelist. 'And there are precious few,' he
was insidious enough to add.

As a result I found him highly interesting. It is,
I believe, a recognized fact that though you may have
in yourself nothing that particularly appeals to your
neighbor, yet if that neighbor appeals to you, at once
a bond is created. Admiration is like love and like
light, a fluid that affects us unconsciously. And so it
fell about that on the evening of the day on which
I met him on the Route d'Espagne, the effect of
which I speak — unless, indeed, it were some other
— became obvious. He did me the honor to take me
into his confidence.

I remember that evening as never any since. The
dusk had been sudden. The ocean resembled nothing
so much as an immense blue syrup. The sky after
hesitating between dead rose and apple-green chose a
lapis lazuli, which it changed to indigo, and with that
for ballroom the stars came out and danced. To enjoy
their sarabands I had seated myself on the balcony of
the club. It was there he joined me. At the moment

it rather annoyed me that he should do so. I was alone with the Infinite, and I know of no better companion. But all this he appeared to divine, and gravely, in his beautiful voice said:

'I fear I interrupt a tête-à-tête?'

To a remark so spacious in its compliment, what could I do except to express my pleasure? That expression I noticed he accepted as only his due, and presently he began monologuing — a trifle pontifically, it seemed to me — on the avatar and the sheer bliss of believing that hereafter we shall vagabond from sphere to sphere of increasing delights until we reach the peace that passeth understanding.

'That peace will be grateful,' I interjected.

'All peace is,' he answered. 'But on earth there is none. For me, at least,' he hastened to add. 'Would you regard it, sir, as indiscreet if I venture to tell you why?'

A wretched Latin stupidity about nothing human being extraneous slipped from my tongue. But, however stupid, it must have contained the invitation which he sought. In his alluring way he began at once talking very fascinatingly about a fascinating girl.

'Believe me, sir, that merely in raising her arms she exhaled the reason of love. She affected me as no one ever had, as no one now ever can. It was at Dam-

martin I met her first. Among our vieilles chansons
there is one that runs:

> ' "A Dammartin l'y a trois belles filles
> L'y en a z'une plus belle que le jour ——"

'The song, though old, seemed made for her. It
accompanied and announced her. It was part of the
rustle of her skirts. I can hear it now as I can hear
the rustle. For years the echo of both has haunted
me. There have been days without number and
nights without end when it seemed to me that echo
would drive me mad. On one occasion I was convinced it had. But that was long afterward. At the
time she filled my life, or perhaps it would be more
exact to say she filled my dreams. For of my life
she herself had little part. It was the vision of her
that possessed me. She represented the goal in that
eternal steeplechase after happiness in which, shirted
and capped in the colors of hope, we all take part.
Does it not seem to you, sir, that few of us get there?
We either fall by the way or miss it entirely. It was
my misfortune — a misfortune by no means unique
— to have been thrown at the last hurdle. A furlong
more and the cup was mine. Dear God! how I strove
to get it! Perhaps, had I succeeded, it would have lost
its savor. It may be that happiness is what we think
it, but on condition that we think it is what we have

not got. It may be that had she cared for me I should
have ceased to care for her. The fact that she did
not may have been the woof of my love. Paradise
lies always just beyond. The thirst for the unobtain-
able consumes us all. What abysses the human heart
conceals! But pardon me, I am wearying you with
this story.'

'On the contrary,' I answered, 'c'est du Bourget.'

He smiled. Evidently the reply had pleased him.
'Do you care for his work?' he asked.

In any fabric it is easy to pick holes. But when
praise is expected I have found it easier to supply it.
It saves time, labor and breath. 'Enormously,' I
replied. 'But you were saying ——'

'Ah, yes,' he continued. 'Well, you have now the
central situation. At first I was part of the landscape
to her. Presently on that landscape I succeeded in
becoming a blur. She was interested, and had been
since her childhood, as I afterward learned, in a
cousin, a young man named, let us say, De Machin,
but he had nothing, and her people, who belonged to
the small nobility, had less. Now, in your country,
among your milliardaires, I should be out at elbows,
but, everything being relative, at Dammartin I was
rich. As a consequence, when I asked it was given.
But you will understand, of course, what I at the
time did not, that her people forced her hand. Mean-

while her indifference to me, which was patent, I
regarded but as the normal attitude of the unim-
pressed jeune fille. After marriage I told myself it
would be my care and my joy — and what a joy! —
to change that attitude. Sir, I did change it, but
I changed it from indifference into detestation. Sir,
did I but touch her she shuddered. My presence was
torture to her, and that torture of hers was agony to
me. Mais passons. A fairer bride I at least have
never seen. Her face was a flower, her eyes were
songs. In a week the flush on her face had faded, the
light from her eyes had gone. In a fortnight she was
haggard. In a month she was dead.'

My attention had wandered. From that which Mr
Swinburne has catalogued as the golden, remote wild
West, a memory had surged. I was re-living an episode that had aromatized my youth. But at this
climax I started.

'Yes,' he repeated, 'dead.' He raised his hands and
waved them. 'Like that. In a minute. It was the
heart, they said, that poor little fragile heart of hers
which my adoring but awkward hands had broken.
. . . We Latins, sir, are perhaps more emotional
than you. In any event, I collapsed. During the
obsequies that ensued, each minute was a separate
death. Sir, it is said we should hasten to cherish those
whom we love lest they leave us forever before we

have loved them enough. Therein was the bitterness of it. Though in the few brief weeks during which we were together I had cherished her to the point of idolatry, I knew and felt, and it killed me to know it and feel it, that I had cherished her better had I seemed not to cherish her at all. Perhaps then she would have consented to remain, and who knows but that in after years — perhaps, too, of her own accord — she would have put her hand in mine? For there are dreams that come true, are there not? Mine, though, was done. I tried to forget — not to remember, rather — but with grief who shall argue? To exorcise it one of our moralists has noted that there is but Time and Silence. It occurred to me that he should have added Work. I turned to mathematics, as another might to drink. Its problems, indeed, vacated my mind of her, yet, once solved, there in haunting loveliness she stood. "I am damned!" I kept repeating, and ultimately, in a final effort to get away from myself, I took to travel. Sir, believe me, in conditions such as mine travel is as futile as study. Wherever I went I found myself there in waiting. I found her, too, grief as well. Who was it — Ariosto? — that said:

> ' "Da me stesso sempre fuggendo
> Arò me sempre appresso."

'I had journeyed to Valparaiso and from there to

Florence before I realized the hideous truth those
lines contain. The memory of her became an obsession which, battening on me by day, plucked in sleep
at my sleeve, woke me, sat at my side and talked
torrentially of her. Grief had convoluted into mono-
mania, and one day, as I have already mentioned, I
told myself that I was mad — yes, and any one else
would have thought me so, too — for I felt that I
had seen her, or rather I felt that my crumbling brain
had from its ruins projected an illusion of the ghost
of the dead.

'I was then in Florence. The illusion had occurred
in that lovely park that is called the Cascine. It
seemed to me that she passed me there, rapidly in a
carriage; so rapidly that in an instant she had gone.
Abruptly everything grew dim. There came to me
the curious and by no means enviable sensation of
falling from an inordinate height, a sense of struggle
with the intangible and the void into which my brain
seemed to tip. When finally, on the morrow, it
righted sufficiently, I got to the French Consulate,
where I obtained the address of a physician, on whom
I then called and to whom in detail I related the story
I have summarized to you. "I am mad, am I not?"

' "Pas plus qu'un autre," he replied. "Tout le
monde est plus ou moins fou. You may have a de-
lusion or two. What of it? Delusions are very

delightful. What should we do without them? Yours, however, are not very complex. You fancy that you have seen a lady who is dead. In reality you have seen some one who resembles her. I think I can convince you of that. Afterward, if you will but convince yourself of the inutility of grief, you will say bonjour to an obsession. My carriage is at the door. Favor me."

'Driving, sir, as no doubt you know better than I, is the chief Florentine distraction. At the hour when this gentleman invited me to accompany him all the elegance of the Lung' Arno was in the park. Thither we proceeded. Hardly had we reached it when I clutched him by the arm. "La voilà!" I cried. For there, in a victoria with a man whom I knew at her side, sat my wife.

'The doctor smiled, raised his hat and turned to me. "That is Mme De Machin, one of my patients, a charming woman, of whom I shall ask leave to present you."

' "But, doctor," I cried, "De Machin, the man with her, is the man with whom she was in love."

' "Precisely," the doctor, with entire calm, replied, "and a very amiable individual he is. His wife is in love with him too. His wife, though, is not your wife. Your wife is dead. You are not, however, on that account the dupe of an illusion; you are merely forgetting the psychological fact that a man cares not necessarily for one particular woman, but for one particular feminine type. De Machin consoled himself for the loss of the young gentlewoman who became your wife by marrying a lady who resembled her. Affection is merely an instinct when it does not happen to be a habit."

'Dosing me with little platitudes of this kind the doctor ran on. As you will readily believe, they left me unaffected. I was at once firmly convinced that my wife was resurrected, and equally convinced that the conviction was the figment of my disordered brain. But divining the inutility of argument, and fearing, moreover, that did I persist, the doctor might, in view of my condition, retract his offer, I managed to appear relieved.

' "You are a magician," I said to him. "An hour ago I was ready for a straight-jacket. Since then, through your wizardry, an illusion has been ablated. You have but now to enable me to exchange speech with this lady and the marvel of your cure will be complete. Without indiscretion, when shall that be?"

'We had reached the hotel at which I was stopping. "Not later than tomorrow," he answered, and left me at the door.

'That morrow never came. The next day I waited him in vain. The day after I went to his bureau. He was not at home. I left a note reminding him of his promise and asking when I should see him again. In the course of the evening I received a reply appointing an hour on the following day. But of the promise and its fulfillment not a word. In the circumstances there was nothing to do but to wait, and burning with fever I waited. Finally, as arranged, he appeared.

' "All my excuses," he exclaimed at once. "And how are our little delusions today? Entirely evaporated?"

' "And that lady?" I asked.

' "That lady? What lady? Oh, yes. Yes. Yes, Mme De Machin. Yes, indeed. Well, I have not enjoyed the pleasure of seeing her since the other afternoon."

'He was lying. I saw he was lying, and he saw that I saw that he was.

' "Tell me the truth," I muttered.

' "The truth, the truth," he repeated, sparring, as it seemed to me, for wind. "What is truth? — verity to one, error to another, an elenchicism fit only to be concealed."

' "Never from him who is worthy to hear it," I replied.

'He had been walking up and down, throwing his hands about, tossing his head. But at this he stopped

short and looked me in the eyes. Apparently the
scrutiny satisfied him.

' "Worthy, yes," he answered at last. His manner
had changed, his tone as well. He spoke now very
gravely. "But are you fit?"

'Comprehending that only manifest calm could
seduce him, I ran my nails into my flesh and
answered, "I am resigned."

'He opened his mouth, closed it, ran his fingers
through his hair, drew a chair next to me, proceeded
to feel my pulse, and without warning, but with the
same gravity, said, very slowly, "I have the regret to
inform you that that lady was your wife." His hand
was still on my wrist, but it had tightened. The pre-
caution was useless. I had fainted away.

'Sir, an hour later I was in possession of myself and
of the facts. From them it appeared that after the
funeral, De Machin, with the object of securing a
lock of her hair, had gone to the tomb. There something convinced him that she had been prematurely
buried. He carried her off, revived her, and she,
touched by such a proof of love — for it was one —
left with him for Florence.

'According to the law of France, and for that matter, of Italy, my rights were clear. I had but to
demand that she return to my domicile. In due
course that demand I made. But there was a point

I had overlooked. Registered as dead, the registry was incapable of revision. And my wife, though actually living, legally was dead to me.'

He paused, drew out a large cigar, lighted it with studious care, contemplated the stars for a moment and presently, in an everyday tone, inquired casually, as if he were asking the time, 'Do you see any climax?'

The question, joined to his change of manner, seemed to me so surprising that my bewilderment must have answered for me. Immediately, in the same light way, but with an entirely contented smile, he added:

'In your quality of novelist, I mean. If not, should one occur to you, will you — unless, as I fear, I have bored you too dreadfully — will you, when next we meet, tell me how you think such a tale should end?'

He rose, raised his hat, passed into the hall to the door beyond.

At the exit the porter stood.

'Who is that gentleman?' I asked

'That gentleman,' he repeated. 'Why, sir, I thought you knew him. That gentleman is M Paul Bourget, the celebrated romancer.'

Alma Adorata

Alma Adorata

L ES VOYAGEURS pour Paris en voiturrre!'
The call rang musically through the night.
I had forgotten that the train had stopped.
Epictetus was with me. I am familiar enough with
him, but he always seems to have something new to
say. In that he differs from others of my friends.
On a train, he is particularly serviceable. He stimu-
lates your imagination, and that spares your eyes.
But, at the call, I looked up, and then at the door
of a compartment which I was occupying on the Sud-
Express, and in which, thus far on the trip, I had,
to my satisfaction, been alone.

Now a man was entering, assisted by two servants.
They got him seated directly opposite me, and then
from the corridor fetched a lot of rugs and bags
which they distributed about. Presently they vanished. I looked at the man. He was a sallow creature,
with great, burning, black eyes, and dressed with that
absence of smartness that is sometimes the result of
philosophy, but more often of indifference, the which,
after all, is a form of philosophy itself. As I was

inventorying him, I saw that he was inventorying me. As our eyes met, he smiled. Meanwhile, the train had started.

'You do not remember me,' he said, in English. 'Yet, of course, I have changed a lot, and you haven't a bit. I am George Capel.'

'Certainly, I remember you,' I replied; and so I did when he told me who he was. We had been at school together at St. Paul's. That is fully a generation ago. Since then, I had lost sight of him. But as memory raised a latch, and he emerged from behind it, a scatter of reminiscences trooped after him.

I recalled that his people were disgustingly rich, and that, after Harvard, he had been billeted as attaché to our minister — we had ministers then — at St. James's. In that effulgence he departed. I saw him going in to dinner directly after royals, and discussing with them the disadvantages of not being born. What is worse, I saw him purchasing as many trousers as he liked without fear of interference at our docks. I saw the magnificence of this splendor, and nothing more, for, almost immediately, a change in the White House had been followed by a change in our representatives abroad, and, of Capel, I heard nothing further. And now, there he sat before me. Such are the surprises of life and of trains-de-luxe.

'No,' he continued, 'you have not turned a hair.

But, then, what a delightful existence you lead! C'est beau la vie littéraire. Whereas I ——'

He paused, looked out of the window, then back at me, and asked abruptly, 'You know what happened, do you not?'

'After your recall from London?'

He nodded.

I shook my head. It was quite one to me. But Epictetus admonishes us to be considerate. I saw that he wished to talk, to abuse somebody or something, to use me, perhaps, as a sewer, and I proceeded to let him. Presently, from the odds and ends of his speech, an idea glimmered. By way of overture, he was executing a fantasy on St. Paul's.

'You remember Manners, do you not? He was in the sixth form when we were in the fifth.'

'Yes,' I answered, 'I do remember Manners, and I remember, too, that he had precious few of them.'

'Candidly, he was a brute. That, though, is a detail. After leaving London, I met his sister. How did you feel when you first read Victor Hugo?'

'Sunstruck.'

'Precisely. That is the way I felt when I first saw her. In London, I had seen beauty by the acre. But not beauty such as hers. The charm of it was so heady that I reeled. I cried "Gloria!" and my heart answered, "In Excelsis!"

He stopped again, and again looked out into the night. I ventured to prod him.

'Well?'

'Well,' he answered, at last, but remotely, as though returning from some inordinate distance; 'well, I had cut Manners long before. There was one difficulty, for their parents were dead, and she lived with him. How I bridged that is immaterial. But I did bridge it. Then, I encountered another difficulty. She was engaged. Meanwhile, she treated me as though I were part of the landscape. There was about as much chance of my getting her as of becoming Emperor of the French. Do you mind if I smoke?'

'Not in the least.'

'Eh bien alors, voilà la situation,' Capel continued, when he had found and lighted a cigar. 'But there are miracles. By the way, do you believe in ghosts?'

'Everything is possible,' I replied. Yet, as I handed out that platitude, I minded me of a lady who, being asked the same question, had answered, 'No, but I am dreadfully afraid of them.' I am quite as much afraid of bores. I did not say so to Capel, however. Frequentation with Epictetus makes one very civil.

'Yes,' Capel retorted, 'yes, everything is possible. You are right — perhaps even more so than you fancy; perhaps more than any one could fancy. For, ultimately, through circumstances which would take

me too long to disentangle, there occurred nothing
less than a procession of miracles. In the first place,
she consented to permit me to vacate the landscape of
which I had been a part. There was miracle number
one. Then she broke her engagement. There was the
second miracle. Finally, she put her hand in mine.'

At this climax, Capel, in a crescendo of triumph,
stared at me through his great, black, burning eyes.

'Ah,' he ran on at once, 'ah, the sheer intoxication
of the bewilderment of it! The past became a mirror,
mirroring nothing save the dream of the coming of
her. The future grew wholly solid, brutally beautiful,
dreamless and real. While, as for the present, there,
fairer than the desire of a fallen god, she stood, her
hand in mine.'

In the excitement of the retrospect, Capel, with
magnificent unconcern, flipped the ashes from his
cigar partly over himself, partly over me. But, at
once, noticing his carelessness, he apologized and
asked would I do him the favor to call his man.

I looked out in the corridor. The servants were
seated there with the porter. I beckoned to one of
them.

'A boire, Ferdinand,' said Capel, when the man
appeared.

'Monsieur désire-t-il à manger aussi? Il y a des
cailles en aspic.'

'Will you eat anything?' Capel asked of me, and, on my thanking him, ordered some mandarin liqueur which Ferdinand presently produced in a flask of gold, and, arranging the little table, with which these compartments are supplied, set it there between us, and with it two little cups, also of gold, which from the workmanship I judged were Deccan.

At Capel's invitation, I took a taste of the liqueur. For a wonder, it was not the imitation. Capel tossed off, one after the other, two of the little cups, and began with his tale anew.

Yet something, the story, perhaps the country through which we were passing, or both, evoked a memory, and, losing myself in it, I ceased to listen.

When, at last, I caught up with him again, I found he had been telling me of the wedding. From what I gathered, it had occurred out of town — at Lenox, perhaps — and, immediately after, he and his bride had driven to the station. On the way, they were run into. Whether by an auto or a trolley I did not hear. In any event, there was a crash. It was the crash that aroused me.

'When I recovered consciousness,' Capel was saying, 'they were carrying Alma away. She was dead.'

'What!'

'Dead,' he repeated; and, as he uttered that mono-syllable, in which all of life is resumed, he looked

down, and in those great, burning, black eyes of his
I divined that there were tears.

For a while he sat, his head still bowed. The guard
entered, offering to make the beds. I waved him
away. But, at the interruption, Capel looked up at
me again.

'You will, perhaps, understand what it meant. At
the moment she was mine I had lost her. For a shock
such as that there is nothing earthly that can palliate
or console. My whole life had gone down with hers.'

'I do understand,' I answered. 'Many another
would have followed her.'

'And do you know why I did not? But how could
you know? That which kept me from killing myself
was the fact that I did not believe it.'

'Believe what?'

'Why, that I had lost her! After efforts on my part,
of which the recital is needless, but of which many
were hopeless and all inconceivable, there, just when
I had got her, suddenly, in an instant, without warning or premonition of any kind, from the carriage in
which we sat, from my side, from my arms, she was
tossed into death. It was too abrupt. I could not
believe it. I told myself that it was not true, that it
was a nightmare from which I should wake.'

'Yes, yes,' I threw in, 'I can understand that also.'

'When I was able, I got to town, to the house which

we were to have occupied. There I immured myself. The servants were told never to approach me. Such orders as I had to give I put in writing and threw out in the halls. Months passed, during which I neither saw nor spoke to any one. The nightmare was about me still. I was waiting to awake. "Everything is possible," you said. Awake, at last, I did.'

'Yes, yes,' I repeated, 'I can understand that, too. For sorrow there is but one cure — time and silence. And,' I added to myself, 'some one to beguile them both.'

But the little à part might have been uttered aloud. Capel was too feverishly intent to heed. He was looking now less at me than through me, on some vista visible only to himself.

'I awoke,' he continued, 'to find that it was not true. You must have read De Vigny,' he interrupted himself to remark, 'and you will probably recall a passage in which he speaks of a vault opening in the far blue sky and showing a shaft that ran up through millennia, on through the æons, and up that shaft he mounted, mounted, mounted ever further yet.'

I did not remember the passage, but my interest, that had waned, increased, and I nodded as though I had.

'One night I, too, mounted that shaft. How? Clairvoyantly, like De Vigny, I suppose. But I cannot be sure. I only know that mount it I did, and that there, very near the summit, among cascades of light, cavalcades of beauty, cataracts of harmony, and convulsions of splendor, Alma stood, her arms outstretched. As I reached her, she leaned forward, and down the shaft of azure we sank together, down through lambencies of amber and emerald, deeper and ever deeper yet, through resplendent perspectives, through pulsations of life unto life, deeper, deeper still, through ascensions of immaculate joy, through tempests of forms and farewells, deeper, still deeper through diminishing consonances, through the undulations of tumults, the trepidations of passion, through swooning splendors, through interrupted delights, deeper, deeper still, through measureless abysses, through millennia, through æons, through kalpas of time and of space, deeper, always deeper, further and further yet, until peace slept upon us as dawn upon the sea.'

'Il devient lyrique,' I mused.

'On the morrow, when I opened my eyes, it was to the accompaniment of music. I was in my room in town, and at the other end of it, at a piano, Alma sat. She was playing an air that I had never heard. It was the melody of it that had aroused me. I went toward her. As I did so, I could see that she was fairer than ever, etherealized, aërial, quasi-transparent, wholly

divine. As I approached, she turned. The rhyme of
her lips parted ineffably, and she smiled. I took her
hand, or, rather, tried to take her hand, but my fingers closed on nothingness. At this, she smiled again.
In words not articulated, which, however, through
some process similar to that of clairaudience, seemed
to vibrate within me, "You forget, do you not," I
heard her say, "that I am but a spirit now? Yet kiss
me. It shall be the seal of our marriage eternal." At
that, she rose to me, and on my lips I felt the volatile
caress of a perfume.'

Capel had been looking at me, intently. But now
his expression changed to one of inquiry. 'There is
nothing improbable to you in this, is there?' he asked.

I was about to answer that there was, but Epictetus, whom I still held in my hand, restrained me.

'No,' I answered, 'I see in it nothing improbable.
A crustacean extracts from the water substances
wherewith to make a shell. From food a bird pro-
duces feathers. Similarly, an animal creates bone.
These processes are marvelous, yet so common
that we give them no heed. But, in view of them,
it is quite conceivable that a spirit may so utilize
particles and elements of air that materialization
ensues. What you tell me is not, therefore, improbable, and as Alma — I beg your pardon — as Mrs

Capel was your wife, there is nothing improper in
it, either.

'On the contrary,' I added, after a moment, 'quite
the reverse. But tell me, have you suffered from
cataract?'

Capel stared at me, blankly.

'At Heidelberg,' I continued, 'I remember that my
shoemaker became annoyed by the apparitions of
deceased, and possibly defaulting, customers. One
day, when I was trying on a pair of those magnificent
boots that harmonize so beautifully with student
caps, he was good enough to take me into his confidence. Had he been an Italian, I should have coun-
seled exorcism; as he was a Teuton, I recommended
an ophthalmic surgeon. The surgeon, I subsequently
learned, came, examined, and operated. In no time,
those ghosts were laid.'

The stare from Capel's face had gone. He was
looking at me now with diligent disdain.

'But your experience,' I resumed 'is, of course,
entirely different. It accords very perfectly with
many another set forth at length by the Society for
Psychical Research. Moreover, it is directly in line
with experiments conducted by Sir William Crookes.
Ce monsieur n'est pas le premier venu. He is a scientist. As such, he was, a few years ago, honored by the
visit of a young and very pretty spirit, named Katie

King. She sat in his lap, decorated his buttonhole with a rose, and told him all manner of delightful things. Said Sir William, in a subsequent monograph concerning her, "I do not say that such things may be; I say that such things are." Personally, had I been similarly honored, I should have refrained from publishing anything calculated to reflect on Miss King's conceptions of the convenances. But, then, I am not a scientist. Then, too, it may be that Miss King gave him permission. There are women who like publicity. It may be that there are spirits with similar tastes.

'But apropos,' I added, 'permit me to ask you a question. We have agreed, have we not, that everything is possible? Let us also agree that everything is explicable. There is no such thing as mystery. There is only ignorance. Now, what I should like to ask is this: May it not be that some of your friends, alarmed by your claustration, and seeking, perhaps, to divert you, succeeded in introducing into your house some — some fairy, let us say, who was fortunate enough to possess a resemblance to your wife?'

From Capel's face, the high disdain had gone. In its place had come that rapt look which mediums share with the insane. Whether or not he had heard my query, I could not tell.

'When Alma kissed me,' he resumed, 'the music

continued, the melody, too, of her inaudible words.
It was all quite real — as real, that is, as the intangible can be. There she was; I was kneeling to
her, gazing up in her eyes, watching the changing
rhymes of her mouth, dazzled by her beauty, trans-
ported by her presence, idolizing her with an idolatry
no mortal heart has known before, yet unable to
touch her, unable to get more than the savor of her
perfume on my lips. Real, did I say it was? It was
insensate.'

'No,' I objected, 'not that. You had all the rap-
tures of love, with none of the disillusions of life —
l'ivresse du baiser sans le contact des lèvres. And
that, believe me, is the ideal. But, if I may ask without indiscretion, did the materialization prolong, or
was it renewed?'

'Every day she came to me, sometimes every hour.
With colored vapor she reproduced herself, reproduced the gown, the lace, the pearls, the flowers
which at high noon she had worn that day in church.
Were it not that instead of the silk of her mouth my
lips met nothingness — at most but the subtlety of
an impalpable perfume — the illusion of her presence
would have been complete. At a little distance, her
translucence was barely apparent. Though but a
vision, she was a distinct delight — to my eyes, at
least; to my heart as well. But, otherwise, the fable

of Tantalus was accentuated, augmented, and mul-
tiplied a thousandfold. To behold her near me was
beatific, but to be unable to hold her to me was torture sublimated and distilled. It was torture so acute
that one night I sprang at a pistol, thinking that in
death, thinking were my flesh thrown aside like a
garment, I could mingle my spirit with hers. Instantly, she was at my side, compelling me to desist,
warning me that I was separating myself from her,
not forever — no, not that — but until I returned
in the Ship of the Thousand Years.'

'What is that?' I asked. 'I have never heard of it.'

'Nor had I. Nor did she explain. She was not permitted to, she told me later. But the threat of it
sufficed.'

'Et puis?'

Capel waved his hands. 'That has been my life
since then. She is always with me when I am alone,
that is, and, save an occasional journey taken, as this
is, at her wish, alone I always am.'

The train was stopping. Through the door of the
compartment the porter peered.

'Bayonne! Dix minutes d'arrêt.'

Capel started. Yet, that was natural. From the
uplands of the occult to a southern prefecture, the
distance is appreciable. He had been far away; I,

too, and to change the air I got up and went out to the station beyond.

There it occurred to me to enter the buffet and order a mazagran. As I passed into the restaurant, a cry followed me, succeeded immediately by the noise of hurrying feet. Turning, I saw a gathering crowd of guards, officials, passengers. I got among them. Capel appeared to have fallen. His servants were lifting him back into the car.

'It is a syncope,' said Ferdinand, in French, when we had him stretched out in the compartment, 'one of the attacks to which he is subject. Jules,' he added, to his comrade, 'telegraph to madame to meet us.'

'Jules had better stay here,' I said. 'I will attend to the message. To whom is it to go?'

'To his wife, monsieur; to Madame Capel, 11 bis, Avenue Kléber. Monsieur is very kind.'

'To his wife!' I exclaimed. I felt as though I were having a syncope myself. 'I thought — I thought ——' Truly, I did not quite know what I did think. 'He is recently married, then, is he not?' I managed to ask.

'But no, monsieur. Monsieur and Madame Capel have a son who is going on his eighteenth year.'

Thereat, at once, in reply to my heightening and

manifest bewilderment, Ferdinand answered me in a manner eminently discreet:

'My master has perhaps been divagating to monsieur. A year ago, he was injured in the explosion of a launch. He hurt his spine, and' — as the man spoke he touched his forehead — 'it upset him here. Apart from that he is as good as bread. Et d'une douceur! C'est un enfant.

'Ah! voilà. J'y suis.'

I looked down at Alma's adorer. He seemed to be recovering — to be returning rather to that world invisible and fantastic in which poets and madmen dwell.

Such are the stupidities and vulgarities with which the rest of us are surrounded that I envied him the unreal that was real to him. 'Cheat yourself and dream,' said Epictetus. Capel had known how better than I who have frequented that sage. He had known how better, perhaps, than Epictetus himself. There was indeed reason to envy him, a thousand reasons to envy his immaculate and imaginary amours.

And, reflecting that of all traveling companions — Epictetus included — lunatics are the most stimulating, I went back to the station, dispatched the message, and got aboard again, as the guard called through the night,

'Les voyageurs pour Paris en voiturrre!'

The Princess of the Sun

The Princess of the Sun

A LOS piès de U.'
From what abyss of memory I dragged the phrase the Lord only knows, but I got it out by virtue, perhaps, of what poets and gamblers call inspiration.

The lady to whom I addressed it bowed gravely, deeply, distantly, with that swanlike movement which has never been customary here and which is not now frequent abroad. It is a form of greeting that belongs to an elder day. But it is very fetching. I was properly pleased, and I should have renewed the expression of my homage but my host prevented. Offering the lady his arm he led her, myself in leash, to the dining-room beyond.

My acquaintance with both these people dated literally from that moment. I had never set eyes on either of them before. A few days previous I had left at this house, which is in upper Fifth Avenue, a letter of introduction that had been furnished me, beneficently, by one of those charming people whose names you may read in the papers every day of your life and who form what is colloquially known as the smart set. The furnishing of the letter had come about in this fashion.

I had been furiously at work on a book of the kind which when published is handsomely bound and never read. The subject had, however, absorbed me. It concerned the Incas. I knew nothing at all about them, but I had found that the best way to master a subject of which you are ignorant is to write it up.

To that end I had haunted the Astor Library. Yet in my séances in those halls there were impressions, fugacious, elusive, which I just discerned and never got. To use a technical term, the atmosphere was lacking. There was not an ounce of local color in the shop. I wanted it by the pail, and there had come to me a foreboding that in search of it I might have to go to Peru.

I hated the idea of that. It is a beastly trip. Besides, at Palm Beach there was at the time a young person with whom I had interchanged all those lovely vows which mean so much and also so little. By every other post I was receiving assorted insults from that girl. It was inconceivable to her then, and has been since to me, how I could prefer the society of dead Incas to her own liveliness. And she suspected, and made no bones about saying so, either, that it was all gammon, that the Astor Library was a blind, that I was engaged on something unfathomably nefarious, and that if I did not drop it and come at once I need not come at all, et voilà, et cetera, and so forth.

I was, therefore, in what I think I have seen described as a quandary. To literary people writing a book is like having a baby. Any interruption in the process is at the expense of the child. Girls never understand that. Though you be willing to give them everything you have and more, too, except one thing, your time, your time is the one and only thing that will content them. Girls are very unreasonable. This young person was extraordinarily so. It was one of her charms, and of charms she had many. So many, in fact, that I did not want to lose their possessor.

I was therefore up a tree. I knew that in sitting about at the Astor Library all the local color I could fish would find a large and ample playground on the head of a pin. I knew, too, that if I presumed to go to Peru nothing earthly would convince that girl that I was not an out-and-out criminal. Meanwhile there was the baby, or, rather, the book, and what was I to do?

At this juncture Providence so ordained that I took tea with the Le Grand Waldrons, who, as you know, are society folk of the toppest notch. These people poured balm all over me. More for conversation than comfort I explained my difficulties and immediately they had a cure.

'I tell you what I will do,' said Waldron. 'I will introduce you to Don Ruis Ixar.'

'You will not have time, dear,' Mrs Waldron interrupted. 'We leave for Aiken tomorrow.'

'Well, I will give you a note to him, then,' Waldron continued. And he did, explaining while he was writing it that Don Ruis was a Peruvian, very eccentric, very rich, very artistic, the very man to tell me everything.

'Particularly about that woman,' Mrs Waldron had interjected.

'What woman?' I had asked.

'Nobody knows. She was at the opera with him last night. The whole house was staring at her. She is a most extraordinary-looking creature.'

'She is devilish good looking,' Waldron corrected. 'Here,' he presently resumed, 'is the note.'

It was as a result of this note that a few evenings later I found myself going in to dinner behind the lady at whose feet, through some prodigy of memory, I had been able to precipitate myself.

When, a moment before, I had entered the drawing-room, she was seated at a piano. At once Don Ruis had come to me, welcoming me in French, then he had turned to this lady, taken her by the hand

and, addressing her in Spanish, had presented me to her.

As he did so I realized at once that in all my life never had I seen, or dreamed of seeing, a human being so exquisite. She displayed in their perfection the three great feminine desiderata — perfect figure, perfect features, perfect grace. Her eyes were pools of purple, her hair was a garland of flame, her mouth a scarlet thread.

By comparison the young person at Palm Beach, whom I had regarded as a pocket Psyche, would have, had I thought of her, looked rather plain. But I did not think of her. On the contrary, mentally I was submerged by this woman's beauty, which from beneath the chandelier under which she stood, radiated with a light so unique that I was in doubt how to define it. It seemed to me to belong to a type of civilization more effective than our own. Mentally, as I have said, I was submerged, but optically I was dazzled. About her were suggestions of the celestial and with them evocations of the damned.

I throw that in not because I think it sounds well, but because I felt that she was a realized ideal. Yet, though I felt that way I could not very well tell her so. In the first place, my knowledge of Spanish is limited to six lessons which I received in boyhood

from a German, and in the second place I am slav-
ishly conventional.

'A los piès de U.' (at the feet of your Grace), was
all I managed to get out, and how I did that the
Lord, as I have said, only knows. Then she had
bowed, gravely, deeply, distantly, but with ineffable
charm, and on the arm of Don Ruis had proceeded,
I following, in to dinner.

The table was a pleasure to look at. The cloth
was gold. The plate was gold. For centerpiece there
was a gold tree, in the golden branches of which
there were apples of gold, the golden fruit of the
Hesperides. The lusters were gold, and in dishes of
gold were golden flowers.

It was all quite agreeable. So, too, was the dinner.
At the latter, which a squad of lackeys served, there
presided the high gastronomic muse of Savarin and
of Brisse. There was, for instance, a strawberry soup
the like of which I have never eaten out of Peters-
burg, and rarely there. For roast, too, there was a
delight. Instead of the inevitable canvasback there
appeared a royal cygnet, the neck arched, the
feathers replaced, an orchid in its beautiful beak.
For sweets, apart from this lady, who was gowned
deliciously and, I assume, extravagantly, though I
cannot be sure, for I lack the huckster's eye — apart
from her there was but a single dish, zambalione, of

which the constituents are plovers' eggs beaten with champagne into an ethereal foam.

During the progress of these and other courses equally classic Don Ruis held forth very amiably and delightfully on the subject of nothing at all.

Mephistopheles is supposed to be slim. Fancy him fat and you can see Don Ruis. His eyes were chocolate, and in them was that gleam that comes from secret and intense satisfaction. He wore a mustache and a great beard cut fan shape. Both were black, blue black, specked with gray. When he laughed, as he often did, he threw his head back, the mouth open, and in the latter I saw that his teeth, after a curious South American custom, were filled with diamonds — with little diamonds, of course. On the thumb of his right hand he wore a big one.

With that hand now and then, during the progress of the dinner and the interludes of his talk, he took hold of the wrist of the lady and, bending forward, addressed her caressingly in his caressing tongue.

On such occasions she would turn to him gravely, leisurely, with that grace with which she had bowed to me, and answer him briefly with the 'Si' which is 'Yes' in Spanish.

Don Ruis ate largely. The lady let dish after dish go by. Infrequently she raised a glass to her mouth and touched her lips to it. Over the soup I had addressed to her in French some observation. Before she could reply Don Ruis answered in her stead, and from the subject passed to others, holding forth, as I have noted, very agreeably.

When the zambalione had come and gone I addressed her again.

'Do you not speak Spanish?' Don Ruis interrupted.

'Alas!' I exclaimed, looking not at him, but at her. 'Alas! all I know is a bit from one of your singers:

    ' "Por una mirada un mundo! Por una sonrisa un cielo!
      Y por un beso! Yo no se que te diera por unbeso!"

'which being interpreted means: "For a look, a world. For a smile, a heaven. And for a kiss! I do not really know what I could give you for a kiss." '

The recitation was not in accord with my usual slavish conventionality. But something, the wine with which the squad of lackeys kept refilling my glass, the woman herself, the vistas which she evoked, all these things, perhaps others, too, must have affected me. Yet barely had the words slipped out before I was conscious of their stupidity.

I was about to say as much, to protest rather, that in letting this thing go I had done so as a beast of a parrot might; but immediately Don Ruis, bending forward again, grasped the houri by the wrist.

At that, quite as though my bad taste were another homage, she bowed to me, while he, throwing himself back in his chair, laughed longly as he bawled out 'Bravo!'

Thus encouraged, I might have fumbled in memory for more stuff of the same kind, but the lady was rising. On the arm of my host she passed through under portières which lackeys held open.

There he bowed to her, the portieres fell, he returned to the table, where we both resumed our seats, and where presently I succeeded in extracting from him whiffs of the atmosphere for which I had come.

Don Ruis talked with a profusion of gestures, volubly, picturesquely, but so abundantly that under the douche of words my interest, already distracted, waned a bit and my thoughts veered from Peru to the supernal loveliness of that woman.

Who could she be? I wondered. Manifestly she was not his wife, otherwise he would not have taken her in to dinner. Manifestly, too, she could not be a relative. He was black as hate, and she was fair as hope, fairer even, so fair that it pleased me to think that she might be an Inca, some ultimate descendant of the Princes of the Sun that ruled Peru with blinding splendor before the Conquistadors chanced that way.

Into the core of that fancy perplexity came. I

began to conjecture where and how I could manage to see her again, and I determined to cultivate Don Ruis, to be insatiable of color and atmosphere, to haunt him and his house on the chance of a word with her.

'Ah, but,' he was saying, 'I mind me now I have pictures of Cuzco — Cuzco, you know, the Sacred City of the Sun. I have pictures of the coraquienques, the sacred peacocks. Yes, I mind me I have pictures of all of these. Your permission. I will fetch them.'

Rising from the table, Don Ruis passed through a door that led, not into the drawing-room from which he had come, but into some other part of the house.

As he disappeared I turned and looked at the portières behind which the beauty had vanished. Long since the servants had gone. The room was very quiet. But from afar I could hear the voice of Don Ruis. He was singing an air from some opera, one of Verdi's, I thought, but which? Then suddenly from behind the portières came a noise, slight yet noticeable, a noise much like to that of a chair overturned.

From beyond there filtered the voice of Don Ruis, 'La donna e mobile.'

It was 'Rigoletto,' I told myself, that he was singing, and telling myself, too, that I might perhaps enjoy a moment with the other donna, I got from my seat, and, brushing the portières aside, passed into the adjoining room.

There I looked in vain for the gorgeous Princess of the Sun. The room apparently was empty. Toward the further end of it the projection of a grand piano, at which she had sat when I first entered, masked a corner, and, thinking that perhaps she might be there, I went forward.

To my unutterable surprise, there immediately I beheld her on the floor, flat on her back, the skirt of her dress disordered, an overturned music stool beside her.

It was, of course, at once obvious that she had fainted. Instantly I was looking down at her exquisite face, from which, to my astonishment, her purple eyes stared up.

'Can she be dead?' I cried.

But no, that I saw was impossible. The scarlet of her mouth was as vivid as before. In her face and the lobes of her ears the pink flush of breath and life was present. Yet still her eyes stared up at me.

In my heightening bewilderment I bent down.

'Madame!' I called. Then tentatively I took her hand. It was cold and rigid, very hard, with a hardness that no hand has ever had, and as with a shudder and a strangled shriek I dropped it I divined rather than detected that this Thing on the floor was not human.

At the moment my brain seemed to tip. To steady myself I turned and clutched at the piano, and as I turned Don Ruis, singing still, erupted.

To have saved my life I could not have spoken, but at that Thing I pointed.

'Eh? What?' said Don Ruis in answer to my gesture. 'Eh? What?'

But at once he, too, saw, and, throwing back his head, the diamonds glittering in his fangs, the brute laughed long and loud. It was a laugh like to that which Swinburne has catalogued as heard in hell, far down. And still he laughed. But at what? And why? Was I mad? I asked myself. Or was he?

'Ha! ha!' he roared. 'Ha! ha! ha! Por una mirada un mundo. Por una sonrisa un cielo. Ha! ha! Forgive us, dear sir. We did not mean to affright you. Our little beauty has merely run down. One moment. You shall see.'

Thereat, drawing a key from his pocket, he got down on the floor, inserted the key somewhere in the waist of the Thing, gave it a twist, another, a dozen perhaps, and stood up, raising with him that which I had taken for a houri, an Inca, a Princess of the Sun, and which I then saw was a mechanical doll.

'How delicious!' I exclaimed. Abruptly my amaze-

ment had departed. In its place delight at such perfection of workmanship had come. 'How delicious!'
I repeated.

'Is it not?' Don Ruis answered appreciatively. 'Is
it not? And, believe me, so very agreeable to have
about the house. The phonograph in her throat only
says the things that I like to hear. Where is the
woman who would be so particular? And no cause
for jealousy, not one. But for envy! Ah! that is
another guitar. At the opera, where I take her; in
the park, where we drive, every man who sees her
looks as though he could eat her up. And the fine
ladies, they are green. Yes, green. Aren't they,
Mariquita?' he added, turning to his doll.

'No, believe me,' he continued, turning again to
me, 'with her I have peace.'

As he spoke he tossed a hand in the air as though
waving away unhallowed reminiscences of women in
the flesh.

'No,' he resumed, 'she is like the rose, she charms,
she does nothing but that. And so docile! A squeeze
of her wrist and my way is hers. But come, Mariquita will come, too, and we will look at my pictures
of Cuzco and the sacred peacocks of the Sun.'

'Thank you, Don Ruis, thank you,' I answered, for
by this time I was tired out. 'With your good leave I
will come another day.'

'At any time. It will be always a pleasure. Mariquita!'

Grasping the doll's wrist with one hand, with the
other touching a button, he summoned a servant to
see me out.

'Mariquita!' he repeated.

And as I bowed to Don Ruis, Mariquita bowed to
me gravely, deeply, distantly, with the swanlike
movement I had admired so much.

And I, not to be outdone in courtesy, repeated, as
I backed to the door, my initial salute:

'A los piès de U.'

The Dear Departed

The Dear Departed

I

ONE by one the guests had gone, and with Trella now there was but a poet who had elevated rhyme to the dignity of a sport. His name was Villiers. In addition to rhyme and other gymnastics less violent, he cultivated paradox. At the moment, he was twisting his painted fingers, fumbling his hostess with his yellow eyes. Then, pontifically, he addressed her:

'There is but one enduring delight — certainty in love. Certainty that it exists, certainty that it is returned, certainty that it will never diminish.'

Trella looked at him so fixedly that he tacked.

'The idea suggests itself,' he hastened to add, 'in connection with the Infanta of whom we were talking at dinner. Nobody seems to recognize that the one to blame for her conduct is her father. Don Carlos is a most ordinary person. He goes about talking, "God and my country," by day, wrecking households at night, as ignorant of Molière, as my masseur. Evil exists only in the noise that it makes.

' "Et ce n'est pas pécher que pécher en silence.'
'Le scandale du monde est ce qui fait l'offense."

'Have you been hearing things about me?' Trella interrupted.

Villiers promptly assumed the appearance of an idiot.

'Do you believe them?' she asked.

He waved his painted fingers. 'Dear me!' he exclaimed. 'I have heard so many lies concerning myself that how can you expect me to believe the stories I hear of others? No,' he continued, remotely, 'had Don Carlos only known enough to cram Tartuffe down the girl's throat she might not have carried on as she has. And then, again, she might have. Bad taste is in the Bourbon blood. The Princess Isabelle let herself down thirty feet out of a window, and ran off with a Polish mucker. They were caught and married by main strength.'

Trella patted a yawn.

'Tell me of yourself,' he agilely added. 'What have you been doing? Or, rather, what have you not been doing? Do you know, I should love so to put my ideas of you in a poem. For private circulation, of course. It would have to be, wouldn't it, unless it appeared in Latin?'

But, as for all reply she smiled indifferently; the

poet stood up, and, balancing himself on his heels,
smiled, too.

' "Our Lady of the Immaculate Conversation,"
would, I think, be a very good title for that poem.
Bonsoir, belle dame.'

Raising her wrist, he brushed it with his lips. In a
moment he had gone.

As he passed from the room a servant entered. On
a little tray he had a telegram which he brought her.
Dated London and addressed to the Countess of
Cloden, Avenue Marceau, Paris, it contained these
words: 'Will be with you tonight.'

With a gesture, she dismissed the man, and, leaning on a mantel, stared in a mirror, stared through
it into the past, stared beyond it into the future, and
then at herself, at her royal beauty, at the sunburst
of flesh which she was.

In all our great Northwest, her grandfather, Com-
modore Verelst, had been accounted the richest and
hardest of men. As a lad he tracked muskrats in the
Michigan marshes. As a man, he constructed and
commanded a fleet of lake steamers. As a corpse, he
left millions. He had one son, who took them all,
took them away to New York, and married. The
result of the union was Trella. The original Verelst
was a German, his wife was French. There was the
gold of the Rhine in the glisten of Trella's hair. In

the faint umber of her skin, in the mobility and droop of her lips there was France. When Teuton and Latin combine there can be some very fetching results. Witness the Venetian. But when to these elements is added the magic of Manhattan the result not merely fetches, it astounds. Trella developed into an astounding young person.

As a girl, she reminded you of what the Argive Helen may have been in her teens. Her mouth seemed to promise more than any mortal mouth could give. Her voice was so insinuating that it conveyed the sensation of a kiss. She had glances as she had intonations, which dispensed a charm quite incandescent. Her eyes were particularly enthralling. They were large and blue, blue as the sea and bluer. Generally, she was prudent enough to keep them half closed. When she opened them they revealed a number of things — curiosity, restlessness and that je-m'enficheisme which is mistaken for frankness. When she chose, she could flood them with languors. She just lacked being tall.

In the process of the production and development of these witcheries her father concluded to leave for another world. After a proper period of regret, his widow left for another world, also. But it was Europe she selected. Though a New Yorker by birth, and inordinately rich, she had never succeeded in forcing certain portals. Such things annoy a woman. Hence the migration.

The migration effected, Mrs Verelst discovered that to be decently lodged, two domiciles are obligatory. Mrs Verelst took three. One in Paris, one on the Riviera, and one in Normandy. To these she added a fourth. The last was a cemetery. Her residence in that resort was not, however, immediate. She waited for certain things, primarily until her daughter was married.

It was on the Riviera that the preliminaries to this event occurred. Entrance to the penal colony, which is called Society there, is a matter of entire ease. Mrs Verelst knocked and it was opened. There was a sesame in her dollars. There was another in Trella's looks.

The particular section of the Riviera which she had selected is, geologically speaking, a Mediterranean cliff; descriptively, it is a sublimate of Paris in a tropic frame; pictorially, it is a fairyland in duodecimo; socially, it is striated with all the variegated hues of beautiful cosmopolitanism, and, familiarly, it is Monte Carlo. You may meet there kings, outlaws, demi-reps, professional beauties, cheap trippers, and Spanish grandees.

In the air is a smell of vitriol and violets, of vice, patented, prodigal, and perfumed. There is not an old-fashioned virtue in the place. There are tears, though, rivers of them, heightened by the click of the ball on the roulette table, the call of the dealers at trente-et-quarante, the music and monotony of Rien ne va plus. People go mad there. Others kill themselves. Some fall in love. Among the latter was Trella.

This extraordinary event occurred in a commonplace manner. At a rout given by the morganatic widow of an emperor the girl and her mother were present. During a pause in a dance, in a crash and subsidence of the orchestra, an Englishman caused himself to be presented. Before speech was possible there arose from beyond the voice of the world's best tenor. It was an aria from the 'Somnambula' that he was singing, the 'Perche non posso odiarte,' which, for sheer beauty, is perhaps the most entrancing in all of Italy's enchanting repertory.

The melting measures proceeded. The Englishman looked at the American girl and she at him. As they looked, the madness of the music seemed at first but the accompaniment of their thoughts, and then at once to transmit those thoughts from one to the other. Involuntarily, he moistened his lips. Into the perfection of the girl's features a flush had come. To use a localism of the land, c'était le coup de foudre.

Trella let her long lashes fall. It was as though she

had dropped a curtain. The man turned to her mother. That lady was whispering something. Yet what, he neither knew nor cared. The measures had swooned. The hush was broken by a ripple of applause.

'It is very warm,' Mrs Verelst announced.

Before any one could engage with her in meteorological observations, the tenor, by way of encore, was distributing the enchantment of his notes anew.

Back of Trella a balconied window opened on the April night. Already she had investigated its possibilities, and raising those lashes again, she led the Englishman to the stars without. The aria followed them. He never forgot that song. Nor, perhaps, did she.

II

Life is packed with pleasures. One of the most delightful is to awake with the consciousness of being in love. On the morning succeeding the rout Shane Wyvill awoke to just that delight. He was turbulently intoxicated by a girl whom he had never seen before, and whose name he did not know.

But the morning was a replica of others. Moreover, it was a family trait to wake up with that sensation. So far back as the family went, and it went as far back as any of the other families which Mr

Burke has so diligently catalogued, the Shane Wyvills — the Shame Wyvills as custom had corrupted the name — had, in love, been freebooters. Titularly lords of Cloden, typically they were a bad lot.

The last earl, after filling the Continent with the uproar of his debauches, gave up the ghost with a shriek. What visions he beheld he lacked the time to relate. It may be assumed that they were not very cheerful. The youth of the existing incumbent had been what the French call stormy. After the storm, the calm. The past twenty years he had passed at Shane Towers, contemplating the landscape. That landscape had been so successfully postobited that it produced less than would suffice for a sweep.

The wants of the earl were many. But they were entirely spiritual. Pending their attainment he sat in a dressing-gown at peace with all the world, including his nephew, Shane Wyvill, who was incidentally his heir.

In the latter's father, hereditary characteristics had been so in abeyance that he had been regarded as a nonentity. He had married one of the Villiers girls, and done nothing worse than lose a portion of her portion in the City. Then he had died, she, also, leaving this heir and what was left of her property. The amount was just enough to enable him to get along on.

Apart, then, from the advantage of being in line for an empty earldom and the further advantage of good teeth and good looks, Shane Wyvill had, from the point of view of the world at large, nothing whatever to boast of.

Even otherwise, he was not of a boastful nature. By way of compensation he enjoyed the formidable repute of being the best-dressed man in London. But the repute was unrighteous. He was too sensible to do more than put himself in the hands of the right people and then forget all about them — except their bills, which he paid, as he paid all such things, on presentation. It will be seen, therefore, that if not boastful, at any rate, he was proud. No one is perfect.

But the imperfections of Wyvill will be the better understood through a showing that this mid-April morning, on which he awoke with the consciousness of being in love, was but a return of sundry others. Fed, as every decently educated lad in England is, on the psalms of Aristophanes, he had also taken a course in Theocritus. In the green pastures of a long vacation he encountered a maiden whose studies had been less elaborate. Their defects he undertook to remedy. One noon he read to her an episode from an eclogue. At its close their eyes met. To quote Dante, they read no more that day. Subsequently, he encountered her, not in green pastures, but in Piccadilly, and at an hour nearer midnight than noon. In the interval she had convoluted into a chorus girl. Her salary was precisely twenty-five shillings a week. At no properly conducted London theatre is it permissible for a lady whose salary does not exceed thirty shillings to drive to the stage door in her brougham. The rule may seem arbitrary, but there it is, and in this case there it was. The young person who perhaps had grown luxurious, regarded it not merely as arbitrary, but awkward. For the sake of old times, Wyvill got her higher pay. Then for the sake of old times, also, she blackmailed him pretty nearly out of his boots. Such was his initiation into the charms of love and Leicester Square.

In politer spheres he presently discovered consolations. These consolations lasted until the lady's husband began uncivil proceedings, from the result of which Wyvill was saved by a succession of events which converted him to a belief in miracles. The lady explained everything so satisfactorily to her husband that the proceedings were withdrawn, whereupon she eloped with another and a richer man. Such was his initiation into the horrors of matrimony and Mayfair.

It is said of those who beheld the mysteries at
Eleusis that thereafter they ceased to smile. Wyvill's
experiences were quite as chastening. The pleasure
in things that had pleased him waned. He tried
hunting, and gave it up. It cost too much. He went
forth to shoot in Canada, and returned disillusioned.
Yet, in default of wealth, one must have a raison
d'être. It was in the search for that raison that he
encountered Trella. Her effect on him was instan-
taneous. Before he slept he was conscious of a new
conception of beauty. When he awoke it was to the
consciousness of a new conception of life. From the
conjunction of these conceptions there mounted like
a flame the delight of a dream of possessing the girl.

In fairyland you have but to ask and it is given.
Since Perrault lived and labored, Monte Carlo is the
nearest approach to that country. In its sorceries are
solvents so surprising that you may land there a
pauper and leave a plutocrat. You may also reverse
the order of things. Where the enchanted rose is,
there, too, is the disenchanting thorn.

But on the slopes which a syndicate in collabora-
tion with nature has strewn with diaphanous days
and electric lights, such thorns as grew Wyvill passed
unheeding, and, in passing, promenaded straight into
the domain of a beauty who, however, was not sleep-
ing, but thoroughly wide-awake.

On the way, Wyvill gathered certain facts, which were so many flowers; the domain's precise position, for instance, its name and the kilometers it took to get there. For even in fairyland, and perhaps particularly in fairyland, there are always mileposts in high hats and others in low neck to provide you with just such information.

In serving Prince Charming they also served the Wide-Awake Beauty. As a consequence, when, in due course, the two met again, had they been first cousins they could not have known more of each other. To Prince Charming the Wide-Awake Beauty was an American heiress, and to the Wide-Awake Beauty Prince Charming was heir to an earldom. What could be more succinct, what more satisfactory? Especially when it is remembered that it had required but one meeting, complicated by nothing more quotable than the melting measures of an aria, for the parties concerned to experience the coup de foudre.

To Trella the coup had all the charm of entire novelty. In New York she had flirted right and left. She liked men, liked admiration and a bold glance, and a squeeze of the hand she was none too shy to return. Apart from a liking for such things, they left her unaffected. After the boldest glance and the tightest squeeze her pulse registered normal. That, however, was less to her credit than to the discredit of the glancers and squeezers. Their seductions were limited to gymnastics.

In Paris and on the Riviera the liking for men continued, but men were scarce. One look at Wyvill had told her that he was of a different breed. Never before had she met any one with less manner and more ease. Never before had she beheld a human being so perfectly sent out. Never before had a presence impressed her so suddenly and so absolutely. For the first time, her pulse ceased to be normal. For the first time she saw a man, and in that man she saw, also, and for the first time, too — or thought she did — her master. At sight of him she flushed. Why, she did not know. But it seemed to her all very new and inexpressibly delightful.

In spite of which, or, perhaps, precisely on that account, when on the Casino's esplanade, chance brought these two people face to face again, only an exchange of platitudes resulted. Yet, in circumstances not similar, perhaps, but cognate, people do not say what they think. As a rule, they do not think at all. They occupy themselves as best they may in sparring for wind. Such sparring as then occurred was rendered more vigorous than otherwise it might have been by the presence of the girl's mother, who stuck to her, not with any un-American view to the observance of the proprieties, but simply because she had come out with her, and objected to being stranded.

The next day matters were more propitious. Wyvill dined with the Verelsts at their villa, took them afterward to the gambling rooms, and accompanied them home again, where he required no urging whatever to remain for a brandy and soda; no urging, either, to dispense with platitudes. After the good old American fashion, Mrs Verelst made herself scarce, and the two were free to gaze at the Mediterranean moon and then at the avowals of each other's eyes.

As weeds of the sea loosened by one current, stayed by another, mount slowly yet surely before achieving their gradual yet certain ascent, so did these avowals, arrested now by query, again by an objection, rise from the depths of their being and mount to their lips.

From avowals to action no appreciable time is required. In a moment they were in each other's arms; in a week they were engaged; in a month they were married. In fairyland lovers don't dilly-dally.

It was not, though, of course, at Monte Carlo that the marriage took place. Against its taking place at all Mrs Verelst protested vehemently. She had an ardent desire to be the mother of a duchess, and the

Duca di Cherella, a young Neapolitan, whom Trella treated as part of the landscape, had, in that desire, collaborated as ardently as she. Failing him, there were others. Besides, Mrs Verelst, who, as the phrase is, had her police, knew that Wyvill's uncle was capable of living forever. In accordance with a good old American custom, she wanted her money's worth, and a title in futuro did not in the least satisfy her ideas of What's What. As a consequence, she protested vehemently. She might just as well have held her tongue. Trella paid not the slightest attention to her. Seeing which, after another American fashion, Mrs Verelst gave in. The marriage took place in Paris, and after the ceremony, through the scented streets, the bride and groom who had met in fairyland set out for paradise.

III

Love is a fever. Marriage is a febrifuge. That is the rule. This marriage was not an exception. Only its antipyretic effects were not immediately observable. At stations along the route the fever lifted them to chimerical altitudes, sank them to spaceless depths, lowered them deeper, lifted them vertiginously, caught and carried them beyond the earth, beyond the horizons of the known, beyond the confines of the real, disclosing through vistas undivined, those mysterious affinities that similarize the flesh and spirit. In fresh ascensions, the fair, illusory promises of love and life were uttered by them both. In new descents the vain, yet lovely vows, Forever, Never, were interchanged again. And so it went.

The duo is very archaic, but to them it seemed highly original, essentially unique, entirely their own composition. It seemed too capable of infinite variations. Through its interludes the memory of a murmur of other songs once filtered in on Wyvill, and jarred him as an oath will jar. Trella's memories were less resonant. They were pages that girlhood had left quite blank, and at which along the route now and then she stopped and mused. With the refrain of that duo shaking constant stars in her ears it seemed inconceivable to her that such blankness there could be. Whereupon, after considering the past, she contemplated the future. The perspectives looked very spacious.

Meanwhile, impeded by nothing more than a maid and a valet, and delayed solely by a courier and a cargo of boxes, they journeyed circuitously from the scented Bois to the pink and crocus of Seville, and on through the ghosts and treasuries of Spain to its summer court at San Sebastian.

During the journey wherever Trella had shown herself admiration had been ambient. She had trailed it as a torch trails smoke. To that she had been always more or less accustomed. But in Seville, after the good old Andalusian custom, it was manifested vociferously, in open compliments of her mother's handiwork, in shouts of Olle tu madre — hurrahs for that absent lady, which infuriated Wyvill, but which, through their fascinating indirection, delighted Trella, as, indeed, every novelty did.

In Castile, the admiration, while quite as fervent, became less noisy, and at San Sebastian so sedate that it would have been colorless had not chance — a function at the palace aiding — embodied it in the Duke of Thule.

The duke, who had an amiable, aimless way, made up in guile what he lacked in sense. Seen across the room, you would have taken him for Teuton; close to, for a fool. Trella saw but the royal. Barring the Regent to whom she had just been presented, she had never met one before. The encounter seemed to her uplifting. It heightened her in her own esteem.

It was at that juncture that she contemplated the future. The more she considered it the more spacious it grew. Then presently, little by little, one after another the delayed effects of the febrifuge appeared. The duo rang less starlike in her ears. The heights began to assume the aspect of the déjà vu, the ascensions to horizons beyond the known acquired the proportions of undertakings, and the affinities, similar-izing sufficiently, had nothing more to say.

Everything being possible, it may be that, in the course of time, Wyvill also would have experienced the premonitory effects of the antipyretic, but Trella's symptoms, at first unnoticed, then misinter-preted, subsequently evident, yet wholly enigmatic, left him perplexed.

Where is the Vandal that invented marriage? Wyvill put to himself some such question, but long after, when San Sebastian was but a halt in the trip and they were back in Paris again.

This occurred in the autumn. At that time, pend-ing the termination of touches on a house which the girl's mother had bought, Wyvill and Trella were lodged at the Bristol. There, one noon, the duke breakfasted with them. Afterward, Wyvill, with the purchase of some horses in view, joined their owner, the Vicomte de Chose, at a neighboring club, and, by virtue of a previous arrangement, drove with him, at 3 o'clock, to Saint Cloud, where the horses were stabled. On the way, Trella, looking nice enough to eat, whirled by in a brougham. Wyvill turned and kissed his hand to her. But the salute was unnoticed. She had not seen him, and continuing his way, he reached the stables, saw the horses, put them through their paces, and returned to the Bristol just in time to dress for dinner.

'What did you do this afternoon?' he asked, when the soup had gone. Without waiting for an answer, he told her about the horses. 'Ce sont des alezans superbes,' he added — a phrase which he had caught from De Chose.

Trella did not know what alezans were. He explained. Then again he asked what she had done, but indifferently, as a husband may, not out of curiosity, but for the sake of talk.

'Nothing,' she answered. 'After you went out my mother came and stayed here with me until nearly 5. Then I took a turn with her in the Bois.'

'Five is rather late nowadays for the Bois, is it not?' he asked, with the same air of indifference.

'The air does me good,' Trella replied, and let the subject drop.

Wyvill stared at her. Her hair made a garland of gold. Her eyes were sultry, her lips were scarlet. About her throat was a diamond collar. Her bodice was sewn with pearls. Between the diamonds and the pearls there glowed the silk of her skin. Never had she looked more beautiful. In the poise of her head, in her appearance and costume, she exhaled a charm almost intolerably aphrodisiac. She seemed created for love, for life at its fullest, and, as it now occurred to Wyvill, for lies.

The dinner proceeded. A maître d'hôtel after presenting a dish for inspection, superintended the serving of it by his underlings. Covers succeeded each other. Of what they consisted Wyvill did not notice. It had been arranged that he and Trella were to go that night to a première and afterward to the Embassy. This arrangement a remark of hers recalled.

Through the flowers and lights on the table he stared over at her again. When a man loves a woman, it is not an excess of ambition on his part to wish to trust her also. And suddenly a solution visited Wyvill. Might she not have accounted for her afternoon as she had, solely to save him and herself the boredom of the narration of some tiresome occurrence?

The solution was so stupid that it soothed. But even in the process of welcoming it there were incidents unconsciously recalled which trooped out and interfered. There was, for instance, a secretiveness which she had recently displayed in regard to such letters as were brought her. Recently, too, it had been obvious to him that she had preoccupations which she did not wish to disclose, thoughts to which he was a stranger. Moreover, there was that change in her, one that had filtered through such subtle

gradations that only latterly the portent had perplexed.

Those who have suffered from jealousy know that
it is physical, they know that it can no more be
argued away than can any other distemper, and they
know, too, to their own cost, perhaps, that its most
torturesome form comes of thoughts that are hidden,
and emotions they may not share.

To Wyvill the lie returned, but unvarnished now,
and with it that determination to *know* which, in certain crises, is as imperious as famine. But of the
inward tumult he gave no sign.

'What did your mother say?' he asked, leisurely.

By way of reply, Trella contented herself with
shrugging her bare white shoulders.

'And you were here with her until nearly 5?'

Trella nodded.

'Why not tell me the truth?'

At this she started. If he had struck her she could
not have flushed more highly. But Wyvill omitted
to pursue the advantage. At the sight of her con-
fusion there came to him a sense not of anger, but
of sorrow for himself and her.

The maître d'hôtel and his underlings had gone.
Wyvill got from his chair and moved it nearer to
her own.

'Distrust and affection don't hit it off very well together, Trella. If you thought that I was deceiving you, you would think, too, that I was ceasing to care. It may be that you are ceasing to care for me. In that case, how shall I blame you? We cannot command affection. It commands us. Then, too, the quantity of it being limited, some day or other it must give out. When it does, love ends. No effort can prevent it. You have loved me now for a long time — almost six months. Unfortunately for us both, this is not a love affair, it is a marriage.'

He hesitated, hoping for an interruption, for some explanation or protest, but as she sat, tantalizingly beautiful and irritatingly dumb, he bent forward and, probing her with his eyes, very deliberately he asked:

'Where were you this afternoon?'

'I have told you.'

'No, forgive me, you are mistaken, you have not. You told me you were here until 5. At 3 you passed me in the Rue Royale. Where were you going?'

Trella stood up, and with a little princess air which she could assume very well when she chose, she looked him in the face.

'You appear to be cross-questioning me.'

'Ah!' said Wyvill, rising, too. 'Very good. I shall not presume to do so again. But I will presume to call your attention to the fact that you have lied to me. You have lied stupidly, wantonly. Whether the lie was meant to cover something equally stupid and wanton, I do not know. I do, though, know that while a wanton act may be shameful yet human, a wanton lie is shameless and vile.

'What is it, Harris?' he interrupted himself to ask. 'No one rang.'

'No, sir, thank you, sir,' his valet, who had entered, answered, producing a dispatch which he had brought. 'The carriage is at the door, sir.'

Wyvill opened the message. 'Then you may dismiss it,' he ordered.

He turned to Trella. 'You cannot go out, with my permission at least. My uncle is dead. I leave for London tonight.'

IV

Wyvill left Paris in a fury, determined to discover what Trella was up to if he had to employ a detective to do it. In the Channel the fury evaporated. When he reached Shane Towers he was glad he had probed no deeper. When the funeral was over he was glad that he had not questioned more.

As to that he was right. To expect some women to tell the truth is as naïf as to expect them to go about naked. They simply can't. Then, too, there are mysteries concerning them which we may determine to solve, but which if time but intervene we prefer to ignore. Wyvill's attitude was, therefore, perfectly natural. But in upbraiding the lady he had been absurd. There are complaints that are compliments, and reproaches which are testimonies of love.

Some inkling of this Trella probably intercepted. In any event, he was presently urged to return. But to return to what? He was still passionately in love with the girl who but a few months before had become his wife; the beauty and the charm of her were as dear to him as ever, dearer, even, by comparison; for in her place there seemed to have come a woman whom he had never known, and who, though her counterpart in charm, was otherwise a counterfeit.

Presently another letter came. He was urged again to return. But to whom? To Trella? Yes, and at once. The trains and the boats were not built that could take him to her fast enough. But with that stranger who had come in her place he had no concern whatever.

Then more letters came. Some were from his wife, offering to join him, and some were from Mrs Verelst, whom Trella's prompt elevation to the rank and attributes of peeress had entirely appeased.

It was then winter. But the winter passed and the spring came before he himself felt appeased. The appeasing was due to a note from the lady, in which she expressed a wish to explain.

As he read the note he could not but recall other explanations of which he had been cognizant. Yet, then, also, he could not but let them go. Time is a strange emollient. In its mysterious potency it softens without our knowledge. We are unaware that it has been acting on us, and suddenly a whisper, a breeze that passes, shows that it has done its work.

That night Trella received the telegram which was brought to her as Villiers was leaving her house.

Meanwhile she had found herself entertaining and being entertained by all that is best and worst in that curious cosmopolis which is called Tout-Paris. Yet there, even the worst have fits of propriety. Society abroad is very much the same as at home. It is not censorious. Provided a woman lives, outwardly, at least, on good terms with her husband; provided, as Villiers had noted, that there is an avoidance of open scandal, a lady is free to be as unladylike as she likes. With the men, at all times everything goes. Yet, now and then they do object to certain associations for their wives.

Of Lady Cloden stories began to be told. To begin with, she was not living with her husband, and it was rumored that, for reasons, which, however interesting, would not look well in print, he did not propose

to live with her again. Such things dishearten.
Moreover, it is not pleasant for a woman of position
to see that position fade. Men acquire with her an
easy form of address. They bow to her sometimes
when they should not, and again omit to when they
should. Matters had by no means come to that pass
yet with Trella, but unless a halt were called social
dégringolage was on the way.

And now on this particular night, as she stared in
the mirror, at the sunburst of beauty which she was,
it was of these things that she thought.

A step aroused her. She turned, glanced at the
great, bare, brilliant room, then at the telegram
which had been brought. Some one was approaching.
She turned again. At the door her husband stood.
With a little bleat which, if not of joy, was a very
good imitation of it, she moved to meet and greet
him, and at once, before he could speak, with a
volubility to which she had not accustomed him, she
acknowledged that she had been at fault, begging his
forgiveness, relating things which he had never
known, that she had a brother, that the latter had
disgraced himself, that he had got into fresh difficulties, that that last afternoon at the Bristol she had
gone to aid him, and that if she had hid the truth,
it was out of delicacy, and the Lord knows what
else, besides.

She paused, for lack of breath, perhaps. At the moment, from the avenue without, through the open window, came pouring the madness of a song of love. Wyvill had heard it somewhere, sometime, a long while ago, yet where or when he could not recall. Then suddenly he was back again in fairyland. The air was scented with flowers, he was speaking to some one, there was an aria that seemed to help his speech, that seemed to multiply the music of the replies. It was from the 'Somnambula,' of course. He remembered now. Perhaps so, too, did she.

Pretty as a peach, and just as witty, savorous as a pineapple and with quite as much heart, commonplace in everything except in beauty, that aria in filtering through her pulp, must have stirred a memory, encountered a fiber, awakened an echo, for to her face she raised a hand and from her eyes there fell a tear.

Wyvill saw that tear. At once his arms were about her, his lips on hers. It seemed to him that they had parted only to reunite, that the past was a nightmare, that she loved him, that he loved her, better, even, than on the route to Paradise.

V

There are lakes which a breeze from the valley disturbs, but which the high winds from the summits leave unruffled. Then, for no appreciable reason, they reverse the order of things. There are natures that resemble those lakes. You never know where you are with them.

In attempting to display the cumulative incidents of this drama, no better analogy occurs by which to explain the opposite effects that circumstances, relatively identical, produced on Wyvill.

They were then at Deauville. Meanwhile, the stranger had gone, and with her every doubt of Trella. She was charmful, the more so, perhaps, because she had had what is called an experience with her husband, and it is said that experience teaches. Mrs Verelst, who had had something in the nature of an experience also, tried to profit by it in offering to restore Shane Towers, and to maintain the place in proper fashion. At this Wyvill protested. It was, he declared, the gloomiest keep in England. Mrs Verelst paid no attention to his nonsense. Trella, either. Paris had palled on her. For reasons of her own she was glad to evolve from it into what her mother termed her rightful sphere. All this was pleasant to Wyvill. The present was pleasant, also, and the future looked, as the future always does look, even pleasanter. And so the days fell by until, the Grand Prix over, they went down to Deauville.

There Mrs Verelst contented herself with a suite in

a hotel. But for Wyvill and Trella there was a house. This house, known, locally, because of its arrangements, as the Villa Portugaise, squats sumptuously before the sea. It is of two stories. The bedrooms are on the ground floor, the dining and reception-rooms adjoining. Between the two principal suites is a wide hall. One of these suites Trella selected for herself. Wyvill took the other. Both are splendid, and the villa itself is a gem.

It was early in July when they reached there. At that period Deauville is usually delightful. But in August it becomes infernal. The season is then at its height, and to its confluence surges a mob of viveurs and rastas.

Among others who appeared there that year was the Duke of Thule. Yet, owing to an attack of Anglophobia with which France is periodically afflicted, he came incog., as a private gentleman, merely. For the purposes of his sojourn he also had a villa. About it night and day men in plain clothes strolled unobtrusively. So are the mighty guarded.

The royal villa was next to the Villa Portugaise, and there, occasionally, as a friend and neighbor may, the duke dropped in, sometimes in beautiful flannels for a game of tennis, sometimes alarmingly begoggled for a flight in an auto, but always amiable and aimless.

And so the days fell by, punctuated by the diversions of Deauville — dips, drives, dinners, dances,
polo matches, hurdle races and baccarat, but particularly by that general deviltry which, in an atmosphere dripping with ammonia and desire, scented
with caprices and seaweed, those consorts of Society,
wealth and idleness, inevitably produce.

Through the diversions and the deviltry of them
the confidences apprehensible were truffled with a
sans gêne quite idyllic.   In the flow of these confidences there was, apparently, not an honest woman
in the place.   Everything being possible, such may
have been the case.

One night the possibility occurred to Wyvill.   That
afternoon the Prix de Deauville had been run.   He
and Trella had been driven to the course by the
duke.   At the track he left them for a look in the
paddock.   On the way back his progress was momen-
tarily impeded.   Before him were two men.   In a brief
halt which a congestion of the crowd occasioned he
garnered a snatch of their talk.

'C'est sa maîtresse,' one was saying.

'Ah! ah!   Et le mari?'

'Il faut croire qu'il trouve ça charmant.'

But the congestion had diffused, Wyvill passed on,
mounted to the tribune, where, looking down, he saw
two men looking up.   They were raising their hats.

Their names he might have remembered, but he had forgotten their faces. He raised his own hat. The duke raised his. There was a clamor, a scurry, a clearing of the track, a careering of thoroughbreds, a riot of color, a shout, the horses were off, the Prix was being run, and the incident forgot.

Truth is an objective phenomenon. It acts in us and on us like a chemical precipitate. You may have given it no thought, and there it is revealed. That night, apropos to nothing, the incident returned to Wyvill. With it, from the depths of his being, there issued an obsession vague and obscure, something opaque and formless, but which, little by little, took shape and changed from an impossibility into a monstrous fact. Wyvill disowned it, disavowed it, would have none of it. But there it was. Presently the disavowals ceased. In certain conditions we get used to monsters. The soul makes itself at home with what it must.

Wyvill was seated in the library. An hour previous Trella, pretexting some one or other of those many malaises which women always have within beck and call, had disappeared for the night. Latterly these malaises and their coincidental disappearances had been frequent, and in considering them the dialogue overheard at the track returned, but freighted now with significance. The soul may accustom itself to

[81]

what it must, but it will struggle first. We believe less what we should than what we wish.

For relief from the obsession Wyvill got up. He would have gone to Trella. But, presumably, she was asleep. In any event, he divined that her door was locked, and he knew that if she answered his knock at all, it would be but to reproach him with having disturbed her. Even otherwise, what could he say? He had suspected her before, and she had been good enough to overlook that suspicion. She had done more, she had produced a brother. There was nothing to prevent her now from producing a sister. With a lady so resourceful conversation was futile.

Wyvill looked at his watch. It was after two, much later than he had thought. Trella must have been asleep for hours. But the obsession had left him restless as a panther. Through the open window he stepped out to the lawn.

It was a perfect night, starful, silent, serene. From beyond, the recurrent hush and retreating wash of the waves accentuated the quiet, calming him unconsciously, allaying his restlessness, reducing the tension of his nerves. Under their influence he sauntered about the grounds a while, and then, turning back, reached Trella's window.

Through the curtains a dim light filtered. As he looked at it, there was projected on the curtains a silhouette, faint but defined. If he hesitated, he never knew it. The window, undefended, opened at his grasp, and tearing the curtains aside, he sprang into the room, sprang at a man that was there, and, with a blow that would have felled a bullock, struck him between the eyes, hurling him backward against a mantel where, falling, his head struck. It cracked like a nut.

Satisfied but not satiated, he turned to Trella. Before he could reach her, the window had become a passageway. A cry, 'Au secours!' had rent the night, and men in plain clothes that guard the mighty were tumbling into the room.

'Hors d'ici, canaille!' Wyvill shouted. 'Out of here, or I'll brain the lot of you!'

Raising a chair above his head, with all his force he flung it at them, but, deflected in flight, it went crashing against the wall; he was struggling with three men at once, while a fourth, falling at the foot of the mantel, was screaming, 'My God! my God! he has killed his Royal Highness!'

'Tant mieux,' Wyvill, struggling still, threw back. But he was struggling with men who had no wish to struggle, who were seeking and uttering words of pacification.

'On ne veut pas faire du mal à Monsieur le Comte,'

one kept repeating. 'N'est ce pas, Paul? n'est ce pas, Jules? Seulement ——'

With a maneuver which Wyvill had acquired in arguments with bargees on the Isis, Paul went spinning one way, Jules another, their mate rolling doubled in a corner.

'Hors d'ici!' he shouted again. 'Hors d'ici, canaille, et enlevez votre crapule de prince.'

He turned in search of Trella. In the commotion she had vanished. But a door leading to the hall beyond was open, and leaving the men, in plain, and now tolerably tattered clothes, to their duty, through the door he passed to have a word with her.

Without, were scared and huddling servants. Scattering them to their quarters, Wyvill ransacked the house, searched the grounds. All he discovered was that an obsession had fled, and that Trella had got away through the night to her mother. Then, divining, perhaps, that she would regard any attempt to follow her as an excess of civility, he turned in and went to bed.

It was as well, perhaps. For what shall a man say to a woman who has ceased to care for him? That she has cared for him? It is better to let the subject drop. So, at least, Wyvill decided. Afterward he was glad that he had not tried to pursue the conversation further, glad that the dear departed had dispensed with the formality of farewell. And so, in the end, matters adjusted themselves, as, in the end, all matters do.

The next day the lady, chaperoned by her mother, journeyed from France, proceeded to this country and then to the land of the Dakotas, where, on the entirely justified plea of cruelty, complicated with desertion, she solicited and obtained a divorce.

The decree was received with general satisfaction. As a nation we do not approve of these matches. Moreover, through Mrs Verelst, everybody knew that Wyvill was a sullen drunkard, with whom no self-respecting woman could live. Trella was more indulgent. She admitted that Wyvill was not, perhaps, all that he might have been, but she declared that she forgave him entirely. That certainly was very nice of her.

Of Thule she never spoke. The press of two worlds gave it out that he died of pneumonia, suddenly, as mortals do die, but decorously, as royals should. Trella never undeceived a soul on the subject. That certainly was nice of her, too.

The Princess of the Golden Isles

The Princess of the Golden Isles

O BERKELLNER!'
'Zu befehl, Herr Baron.'
It was the dining-room of the Kurhaus at
Eichwald. On arriving I had given the head waiter
a florin or two. Hence the title of Baron with which
he was gratifying me and which, for another florin
or two, he was prepared to heighten into Graf and
elongate into Durchlaucht. During dinner I had exchanged a few words with a man who sat opposite
to me, a tall, spookish person with a face of ghastly
pallor. At the conclusion of the meal he had vanished. But now his face, returning, haunted. I
could have sworn I had seen him before. Yet where?

'Sagen sie mir,' I said to the waiter, 'wer war der
Herr der eben das Zimmer verliess?"

'Ein Französe, Herr Baron, ein Advokat. Er
sheint mir ——'

The waiter ran on into voluble digressions, but
I had ceased to hear. At the mention, not of the

stranger's nationality, for with that, of course, his speech had acquainted me, but of his profession, memory raised a latch, years retreated and I was back in Paris assisting at a celebrated case.

The case, though celebrated, was simple. Some time previous, at one of the Philadelphia assemblies, a girl effected what is called her début. Her name was Mary Asher. In appearance she was slight, very fair, with the features of a cameo. Her mother was a Hemingway, and her father, an Asher of Asherton, was known to everybody as one of Philadelphia's leading physicians. Socially the girl was all right, and financially an heiress.

At that assembly there was also present the Vicomte de Cléry, a young viveur, no better off than the law allows and alarmingly good looking. The girl sat out the cotillion with him and, after the ball, retired to Spruce Street, where she dreamed such dreams as maidens may. The Vicomte had made short work of her. He did not stop there. In a short time he made her Vicomtesse. The pair proceeded to Paris, where they proceeded to enjoy both love and life.

In the process a year passed, then another. Ultimately one morning M de Cléry started out as usual for a gallop in the Bois, returned the picture of health, sat down to breakfast with his wife, tumbled over and died. The grief of the widow was tragic. So also was that of the dead man's mother. But through the grief of the latter a suspicion filtered. At first microscopic as a minim, that suspicion magnified itself into a mountain. As a result, the Vicomtesse was arrested.

To that assembly where Mary Asher had encountered De Cléry I had gone on from New York in a party. There were just forty of us — Forty Thieves, as we were afterward called, and not inappropriately either, for the majority of my companions demonstrated a superior ease in the filching of hearts and partners. But, to pursue the simile, their lay was not mine. I was a looker-on in Vienna, an idler in Italy, an observer at this particular ball. Among the objects of my observation was Mary Asher. I found occasion to be introduced to her, and, though it was her beauty that had allured, her charm detained. That charm resided not merely in her manner, which was refreshing, but in her eyes, which were frank. In their light I could see that if ever a girl deserved to be trusted, there she stood.

Two years later, when I learned of her arrest, these impressions returned. It is abominable, I decided, and, as I happened to be in Paris, I determined to be present when the case was heard.

In that determination others collaborated. The

pretorium was invaded by the street, the court taken by assault. In the tribune were first-nighters, society women, boulevardiers, dramatists, and magistrates. At the bar, on the steps of the judiciary, in the laps of journalists, in the seats of the jury even, were cabotins and criminals. The air was suffcoating. There was not room to budge. The aspect of the place was that of an arena. There was the same avidity, the same cynicism, the same thirst for blood. The riffraff of Paris had flooded the hall as the rabble of Rome filled the circus. And to an audience such as that Mary Asher was tossed like a prey.

I saw her as she entered. In my life never have I seen such an expression of such utter despair. Grief had ravaged her face like vitriol. She could barely walk, and fell, rather than dropped, at the dock. It was pitiful, and the pity which I experienced others must have shared. In spite of the ambient cynicism, a murmur of sympathy circled. To me her appearance was incompatible with guilt. It is the misfortune of a novelist to be obliged to investigate all things, crime as well as virtue, and every real criminal whom I have seen in court has been unabashed, either indifferent or defiant. Mary Asher reminded me of nothing so much as a flower that has been trampled. Near her, Maître Lefroid, a tall, lantern-jawed man, was seated, and, on the same bench, I recognized her father. Both were speaking to her. Their conversation the greffier interrupted. The indictment was being read. At its conclusion the president — the presiding justice — a valetudinarian in a crimson gown, turned and addressed her:

'Madam, I will ask you to rise. You are an American. Your father is a physician. From notes before me contained in your diary I assume that you familiarized yourself with his library. Subsequently you met and married M de Cléry. It was a love match. You accompanied your husband to Paris. For a while, between you everything was sugar and honey. But presently your husband began to neglect you.'

At this, the accused, who stood, a handkerchief to her eyes, bowed her head. She was sobbing.

The president continued: 'For this neglect you reproached him. Reproaches do not reconquer a man. M de Cléry neglected you more. Quarrels ensued which your servants witnessed. On one occasion you were heard threatening him. Scenes of this nature wearied M de Cléry. Finally he affiché'd himself with an actress. Your patience was already exhausted. Then, very suddenly, M de Cléry died. Your grief was such that it became necessary to administer morphine. While you were under the influence of this drug, your mother-in-law discovered among your effects certain things I have here before me. One is your diary. In it, day by day, you recount your disillusions. I will read but two extracts. The first is the copy of a letter which you appear to have addressed to your husband. It is as follows: "If you knew the tortures which you make me suffer, you would weep for shame. You are not so wicked as you seem. At least, I hope not. Yet, if by your conduct you convince me that you are, I shall weep no longer. It will kill me. Oh, Maurice, before I do anything rash, come back to me, for I swear to you that otherwise one of us must die. I am at your feet, kneeling there, calling to you before it is too late, crying to you for mercy." The other extract is limited to a word, one with which I may admit I was unacquainted until I saw it here, but which the jury will appreciate. That word is "muscarine." What is muscarine, madam?'

For answer the accused, who stood, a handkerchief still at her eyes, shook her head. As before, she was sobbing.

'I am not to understand, am I, that you do not know? No. Merely that you do not wish to answer. I then will answer for you. Muscarine is a poison. Its effect is sudden. The mention of it in your diary has a significance which is heightened by this other object found among your effects—a picture of your husband on the back of which you have written, "Maurice, who shall die by my hand." Madam, be seated.'

The accused sank back. The hall, which had been hushed, broke into such commotion that the president threatened to evacuate it. Barring a court officer, no one paid any attention to him. The uproar continued, lulled only by a procession of witnesses succeeding each other on the stand — servants and experts, one of whom testified that muscarine leaves no traces and that the reagents employed in the autopsy had determined only slight discolorations superinducible as well by natural causes as the reverse. Thereat the summing up ensued, whereupon Lefroid addressed the jury.

'Gentlemen,' he began, 'in the years that I have pleaded and during which I have been obliged to probe the depths, often obscure, of the conscience of my clients, I have remarked in women a curious ability to deny evidence, to distort testimony, to embroider facts, to evolve explanations, and to lie — even to their attorney. To get at the truth, I have been compelled to treat them as pathologists diagnose disease, and when at last the diagnosis was complete, again and again I have despaired of their acquittal. But in the present instance my experience has gone for nothing. The lady who sits there had no story to tell me, no imaginary defense, none of those tales which women invent and which, tenaciously reiterated, they end in believing. That lady has been too overwhelmed by death to consider life, too prostrate with grief to harbor fear, too crushed for invention. Gentlemen, they are most hopeless who have hoped the most. The hopes of my client were such that in losing them she has lost even the instinct of self-preservation. Of all human beings I have known, she is the most despairful. She adored her husband, and not merely is he taken from her but she is charged with his murder. It is true she reproached and threatened him. But what are a woman's reproaches but testimonies of love? What are her threats but confessions of weakness? Though a woman reproach the man whom she loves with a hundred crimes, though she threaten him with a thousand deaths, he knows that if he but return, his crimes are absolved; that in her heart always there is forgiveness.'

The address continued, punctuated with applause. The sincerity of the man was obvious, and that sincerity he strewed about him as seed is strewn, full-handed, with increasing conviction. You could see it germinating among the jury, budding into blossoms of commiseration, preparing to flower into acquittal, and that, too, despite the evidence, despite the facts.

Then suddenly, without transition, the sower was replaced by the reaper. With a logic, mathematical in its precision, Lefroid took each count in the indictment, one after the other, demonstrating its nullity, giving to each its proper perspective, winnowing evidence from truth, showing that though muscarine was mentioned in the exhibit, nowhere else had it been found, and insinuating the idea that the accused intended to administer it, if administration there must be, not to her husband, but to herself.

Amid fresh applause, he turned to the dock and addressed the prisoner:

'Courage, madam. That man took everything from you — your youth, your love, happiness and confidence, the dreams and illusions of your girlhood, everything,— yes, everything, even to your money. Freedom will not replace what you have lost. The verdict of the jury will acquit you, but it will not console. Yet, little by little, in the years to come your tears will be dried and peace restored. My task is done. I leave you to these gentlemen, confident in their justice.'

Lefroid sat down. The jury filed out. Presently back they came, and at once, to the accompaniment of a clamor and frenzy and bravos, I caught the

French equivalent of 'Not guilty.' The noise was deafening. Those who were not shouting were clapping their hands. But my enjoyment of it was impaired by women who were using me and the press table at which I sat as a stair to Mary Asher, in whose arms they flung themselves with jubilant shrieks.

And now, as I sat in the Kurhaus, memory raised a latch, the sights and shrieks returned. Yet at the moment the reason of their visit was obscure. It was years since the trial was held, years since I had thought of it at all. In its parade the digressions of the waiter had continued unheeded.

'Ja, Herr Baron,' he was saying. 'Ein Französe, ein Advokat.'

I looked up at his fat, honest face. 'Und sein Namen?' I asked.

'Lefroid,' he answered. 'Der hochwohlgeboren Herr Lefroid.'

The digressions continued. Unconsciously I gathered the fact that the lawyer had come to Eichwald for the baths, which, of course, the Romans had built; and I asked myself, Where is the spot in which they did not build baths? — or, rather, where is the European bath of which the origin is not attributed to them? But the query fainted, submerged in the surprises of memory. It seemed odd to me that the entire drama should unroll for no other reason apparently than because I had exchanged speech with a man whom I had forgotten, and mentally I determined, should the chance occur, to ask him what had become of his client.

The next day I looked for him at the baths and again in the perfumery of a garden where a Viennese band was distributing the waltzes of Keler Bela. But it was not until evening that I met him, and then in the dining-room, where he appeared already to have supped and where he sat, a glass of Voslauer before him. As I took my seat he bowed to me, and presently, after I too had ordered and enjoyed a glass of that splendid Austrian wine, I opened the conversation with the announcement that I had had the privilege of listening to him during the trial of Mme de Cléry.

'She is a compatriot of mine,' I added. 'May I ask if you know what has become of her?'

At the moment he was raising a glass to his lips, but at the question his hand so shook that the contents spilled on the table. Ghastly pale, he seemed, if possible, to grow paler.

'It is my nerves,' he muttered by way of excuse. 'Ah,' he continued, casting about, it seemed to me, in an effort to change the subject, 'you then are an

American.' With that abruptly he got up from the table and left the room.

People go to Marienbad for obesity, to Teplitz for lumbago, for neurasthenia to Eichwald. It is the haunt of mattoids. Anywhere else the conduct of Lefroid would have perplexed me. But at these baths — to which a series of shocks, induced however by nothing more severe than baccarat, had sent me — I accepted it as a matter of course. He has been overworked, I told myself, and, dismissing the subject, returned to Voslauer and pheasant.

Yet, whether it was because of the baths, or the fact that we were both strangers in a strange land, or some other factor as yet unexplained, in any event, as the 'Kur' proceeded my acquaintance with Lefroid so far progressed that presently we got into the habit of sitting together over our wine. He was not very communicative, and manifestly he was very nervous, but when he did talk he talked well. Then it so happened that a patient in the establishment committed suicide, as patients there sometimes do, and that evening conversation turned on the subject.

'Have you ever been drawn that way?' he asked.

'Who has not?' I replied. 'But two things have always preserved me — an interest in political economy and the fear of getting hurt.'

'Stendhal must be a friend of yours,' he answered,

and consulted the ceiling; adding after a moment, yet more to the ceiling than to me, 'Mme de Cléry attempted it.'

'Before her arrest?'

'After her acquittal. At that time — but — but let me see.' He hesitated, paused, raised a glass, emptied it and stared at the ceiling again. 'Ah, yes,' he resumed, 'I remember. It was this way. At that time she was done with life, done with it completely — or, to put it more exactly, she had done with love, and to some women love is life. Having lost the one she had no use for the other. But the possibilities of youth are inscrutable. Then, too, love returns to the heart as the leaf returns to the tree. I told her that. I told her everything that I thought could, if not console, at least convert. At first it was as though I were speaking to the dead — to the drowned, rather, in whom there is still a chance of resuscitation. She seemed to have sunk into the depths where my voice could not follow, into those deepest depths where life is without form, without color, without sensation of any kind. But precisely as I had determined that she should be acquitted, so after the acquittal I determined that she should revive. And indeed, either because of her youth or my effort — because, it may be, of an influence not higher but the reverse, *because she had*

not suffered enough — presently death loosed its
hold, retreated, left her; life beckoned to her again,
caught her, wrapped her in its arms, rocked her,
whispered to her and lured her back into convales-
cence. The possibilities which I had evoked came to
her, plucked at her sleeve, sat with her, displayed
their chimeras, accustoming her to their witcheries,
familiarizing her gradually with their enchantments,
until imperceptibly, little by little, after infinite hesi-
tations, relapses, retrievals, issuing from that con-
valescence, she put her hand in mine.'

'What!' I started so suddenly that Lefroid, who
had been monologuing far more to himself than to
me, started too.

'Sir, it is as I have the honor of telling you. She
became Mme Lefroid. The name is bourgeois, is
it not? You recall her beauty. With that beauty
it clashed. That I decided to remedy. On our wedding trip we went to the Isles d'Or — to Hyères, as
the place is more generally known. It is a charming
spot, and it so charmed her that I bought a bit of
property and, influences at the Vatican aiding,
bought also a patent of nobility which enabled her to
call herself Princesse des Isles d'Or — Princess of the
Golden Isles. You will agree that the title fitted her.
She took in it a pleasure as entire and as innocent
as a child will in an unexpected toy.'

'It is pretty,' I threw in. 'But, how fantastic! It sounds like a reminiscence from a fairy tale.'

'Sir, it was in fairyland we were living. In the dream of it, rather. Yet dreams do not last.'

He hesitated again, looked at me, at the ceiling, perhaps through it at the past.

'Sir, she adored me. However much she had loved De Cléry, she loved me more. The man was a brute. It never occurred to me that his brutality I could exceed. And yet I did. It killed her.'

The Voslauer was having its usual effect and I was getting sleepy. But this climax shook me. It seemed to me that there were tears in it, regret too, the regret that is made of remorse. Here is melodrama, I reflected, and as the article is one of which I am always in search, mentally I bolstered my attention.

'Sir, up to the very last, perhaps even at the very last, she adored me. Her notebook, which I afterward found, showed me that, showed me, too, the anguish of an agony which she concealed from me and which not for a moment did I suspect. No, and for the infamous reason that I was too occupied with other suspicions, with suspicions which, to my eternal perdition, I was vile enough to express. Sir, it was that which killed her.'

He waved his hands. I noticed that the muscles of

his mouth were twitching. But at once he was off again.

'Sir, we were then in Paris. There one day she was obliged to dismiss a servant. She never dismissed another. As I afterward discovered, the reptile thanked her, expressing a feigned joy that he had escaped being poisoned. The venom of that must have affected a nature as vibrant and sensitive as hers. But presently other things added their quota. A case was called for trial, one quite parallel with her own, a woman accused of murdering her husband. The feverishness with which she followed the reports you may imagine. In these reports she saw her own procès mentioned. That was but natural. The two were so similar, yet differing in this: the woman was convicted. The conviction must also have affected her profoundly. But other incidents supervened. Among her acquaintances she noticed that some had become absent-minded, others near-sighted. In receptions at which she appeared, people eyed her furtively, talked inaudibly, whispered together, moved away. These things — others, too, no doubt, of which I am ignorant, for she never mentioned them, never complained — stayed her steps, preyed on her, undermined her health. I saw that always there was present something of which she never spoke. If I asked, she answered at random, alleging fatigue, advancing any one of those myriad malaises which women when they wish have within beck and call. It was as though she were sitting in the shadow with a phantom between us. But why was she in the shadow? What was the phantom? I did not know. Then, from being unable to understand the present I turned to the past, to the day when in prison for the first time I saw her and tried to solve the mystery of De Cléry's death.'

'It was rather odd,' I interjected. 'What was it after all? Heart disease?'

'Sir, he had no heart. After considering his death, I began to consider our marriage. Why had she taken me? Je ne suis pas beau, non, n'est-ce pas? Alors, pourquoi? That pourquoi haunted me. In search of an answer I got out the dossier and went over the case anew. The arraignment seemed to me then convincing enough and my own plea absurd. Between the two her figure surged, but differently from before. A figure composed half of hysteria, half of passion, a woman insatiable of pleasure and, in pursuit of it, irresponsible, monomaniac, hesitating at nothing, even at crime. At once her silence became communicative, her preoccupation clear. In that shadow she was concocting something. The phantom was its success. The Why flew away. In its place came When? As that query leaped into my brain, I shuddered. The shudder was succeeded by fever. I wondered, could When mean Already? Abruptly I ran to her. "What is the antidote for muscarine?" I shouted, and at what seemed to me her feigned bewilderment, "How did you give it to De Cléry?" I cried. "I am not well, I am certain that ——" For reply she looked at me. Shall I ever forget that look? There was in it the heart-rending fright of a child pursued. There was in it despair, agony, something suffocating too; and, abruptly, as I had run to her, with a scream she ran from me. I followed after, but she got to her room, threw the door to, and locked it. When I succeeded in breaking through, she was on the floor, her face convulsed, her mouth distorted, an empty vial at her side.'

'Verzeihen, meine Herren, die gnädige Frau lasst fragen ——'

It was Karl, the head-waiter, who, unperceived by either of us, had approached and was addressing Lefroid. With a word of apology, the latter got up from the table and left the room. As he went, a sense of infinite pity possessed me — pity for him, pity for the fair girl whom he had harried down to death — and for a while I lost myself in the tragedy, in returning and retreating visions of the Princess of the Golden Isles — Golden Isles indeed, on whose sharp reefs her fragile bark, illy steered by him, had foundered. A dozen questions occurred to me. At the moment I contemplated waiting Lefroid's possible return. But it was late, fully 10 o'clock. I too had come to Eichwald for my nerves, and, reflecting that they had supped sufficiently on horrors, I postponed the questions till the morrow and ambled off to bed.

But on the morrow Lefroid was not in his accustomed seat. It was occupied by a very large woman, unmistakably middle-class, a medallion under her triple chin, an expression of extreme decision in her face, and, about the corners of her mouth, a pronounced mustache in gray.

Karl was hovering about, and, calling him, I asked after Lefroid.

In a whisper, with a touch at his forehead, the man informed me that Lefroid was not well, and, bending yet nearer, added, 'Die Dame gegenüber ist seine Frau.'

'Unsinn!' I exclaimed.

The 'dame opposite' must have heard. As I stared at her she stared at me.

'Pardon,' I said in French. 'The waiter tells me

that I have the honor of addressing Mme Lefroid. I have the privilege of knowing M Lefroid.'

The creature nodded and helped herself to some peas.

'May I, without indiscretion,' I continued, 'venture to inquire how long he has enjoyed the advantage of being your husband?'

In the voice of an ogre the creature manipulating those peas with her knife replied, 'Five-and-twenty years, monsieur.'

'Ah,' I exclaimed, now thoroughly flabbergasted; 'ah, indeed. I congratulate him. But last evening he was telling me about Mme De Cléry, the Vicomtesse de Cléry, whom he once defended. She is a compatriot of mine. Do you happen to know what became of her?'

'Perfectly, monsieur. After the trial Mme Cléry returned to the Americas with her father.'

'Ah,' I repeated in a crescendo of bewilderment, through the apogee of which, however, a glimmer of understanding suddenly shot. 'Ah, indeed. M Lefroid, I regret to hear, is not very well.'

'If he were, monsieur, what would he be doing here? You do not seem very well yourself. But in this place'— and the ogress juggled again with the knife —'every one seems off.'

'Ca y est,' I reflected. 'I see.' And with a smile which that creature must have construed into a leer quite as lunatic as any which her husband could display, I decided that my nerves had got all the good they could out of Eichwald.

'Karl,' I called to the waiter, 'die Rechnung.'

'Zu befehl, Herr Baron.'

The Noose Matrimonial

The Noose Matrimonial

MR JONES, mem, is downstairs, and your aunt and your father. Your father, mem, he has been here three times.'

It was Harriet, Marie's maid, talking vainly through the door.

Marie turned on a pillow and carefully, as though engaged in a matter of great importance, made with a hairpin little punctures in it. The room was big and bright. From without there mounted the rumble of Fifth Avenue.

The puncturing of the pillow continued. There was a square, quite even, which she completed, and into which she stuck, one by one, a row of dots. In the middle she planted the hairpin, left it there and turned again.

Because of the silks with which the bed was covered it looked like a garden, and in it the girl resembled a flower, a rose chimerically fair. Her purple eyes were sultry, her scarlet mouth was moist, the red tangles of her hair made a burnous of flame, her fingers glowed and her wrists were such as those on which, in days gone by, falcons alighted and kisses fell.

She patted a yawn and interrogated a clock. It was not yet noon, but she had fancied it earlier. Pushing the silks aside, she got from the bed to the bath. Before the latter was a mirror. For a moment, the point of her tongue just visible, she looked herself up and down. Then absently, her thoughts on other things, she perfumed the water and hid herself there.

The chill aroused her. Presently, without haste, she began to dress. The ceremony was one which she always accomplished alone. The presence of her maid annoyed her exceedingly, and, though this morning differed from all others, it was not until she had her hat on that she opened a door and called:

'Harriet!'

'Yes, mem.' The maid entered, prim as a Puritan Sunday. 'They are waiting for you, mem. Your father ——'

Marie interrupted her. 'Put those things in the bag and give it to Harris with the boxes. Are they packed? How do I look? Go down and tell Mr Usher I am coming. When did my father get here? This morning?'

'Yes, mem.' The woman nodded and turned.

Marie went back to the mirror. Her dress was of

cloth, light violet. It had fur effects that were repeated on her hat. In spite of her coloring, or, perhaps, because of it, it became her. And now, as she
looked, she bent forward and kissed herself in the
glass.

'Good-by, Marie.'

She looked about the room. On a mantel were
some photographs.

'Good-by, everybody.'

Her voice was contralto. As she spoke she smiled
and showed her teeth. They were small, slightly
uneven, and semi-transparent.

On the stair beyond was a man. He looked as
though he had seen worse days and never intended
to see them again.

'I was coming for you,' he began. 'I must speak
to you.'

Marie interrupted him as she had her maid. 'I
expected you last night. How do you like my hat?
Have you seen Paul?'

From an adjoining room a clergyman issued. He
was in full canonicals. The girl went back a step,
stretched a hand, showed her teeth and the point of
her tongue.

'I am Miss Mermex.'

'For but a brief while now,' the clergyman answered.

'This is my father,' she added.

'I am just in town,' Mr Mermex announced. 'I got here an hour ago from San Francisco. I ——'

Marie interrupted him again. She gave him a slight shove, which he obeyed, and down the stair all three went.

In the wide hall below people straggled from the drawing-room to greet her. There was her aunt, Mrs Metuchen, a little old frump. There was her immediate husband, Paul Usher. There was Mrs Usher, his mother. There were the Enevers, society folk of the toppest notch. There was also Alphabet Jones, a man of polite letters.

Mrs Usher's costume indicated mourning, Mrs Metuchen's the Flood, and Mrs Enever's the Rue de la Paix. Marie, fair as an angel, yet, of course, much better dressed, beamed on them all.

Usher took her hand and kissed it. Had he not been a broker you would have suspected him of it. Marie, smiling still, showed again the point of her tongue. It was like a little piece of watermelon. Meanwhile, everybody was talking to her; Mrs Metuchen very shrilly. Mrs Usher approached, gratified her with a frosty caress, and stepped gingerly away.

'Many happy returns,' Jones murmured, seductively.

'Gracious!' Mrs Enever exclaimed. 'Gracious!' she repeated, delightedly. 'What a congratulation to a bride!'

'She reminds me,' Mrs Usher whispered, 'of a beautiful animal. But I have found it well not to be too precipitate.'

'Gracious! I should hope so!'

'Marie,' began Mr Mermex. He had got near his daughter again, but Mrs Enever's husband was talking to her. The girl interrupted them both.

'Suppose we go in.'

The group parted. Through it, into the drawing-room, the girl passed, the clergyman following, the others at his heels. At one end, between the windows, two cushions had been placed. The clergyman got behind them, his back to the wall, and, fumbling in his skirt, produced a book. At once he assumed an attitude that was amiably austere.

' "Dearly beloved, we are gathered together here ——" ' Before him the bride and groom were standing. The others, distributed as for a photograph, seemed reverently disposed. Mr Mermex alone was restless, and, in a moment, as the opening exordium concluded with the mandate, ' "If any man can show just cause why these two persons may not be lawfully joined ——" ' he raised a hand, his mouth opened, something trembled on his tongue. But, save Marie, who turned, smilling still, no one noticed.

' "I require and charge you both, as you will answer at the dreadful day of judgment." '

Marie had turned again. She was listening now devoutly. Into her sultry eyes there had entered an expression almost saintlike. From her moist mouth the smile had gone.

'Paul, wilt thou take this woman ——'

The questions continued. At the demand, ' "Who giveth," ' Mr Mermex made a gesture. Though vague, it sufficed. The promises were exchanged. The troth was plighted. Bride and groom knelt and arose again.

' "Those whom God hath joined," ' the cleric continued, and, mumbling the phrases that follow, concluded with the finishing 'Amen.'

'Let me congratulate you, Mrs Usher.'

Abruptly the man of God had disappeared. It was the man of the world who was speaking now. Then, extending his hand to the husband, he was about to ask for the paper which the Bureau of Vital Statistics exacts, but Mr Mermex gave him no time. He had the groom by the sleeve.

'I want to speak to you.'

'What about?' Usher asked.

'Come from here and I'll tell you.'

With a hand still on that sleeve the father led the son-in-law from the room. In a moment the clergyman rustled and vanished. Marie had seated herself, Enever on one side, Mrs Metuchen on the other.

Across the room Mrs Usher mère had also seated herself. Mrs Enever and Jones were sharing the charm of her talk.

'It is incredible,' she was announcing to both from behind a fan, 'but I am not sure that any one knows my son's wife, that any one knows her father, either.'

'Gracious!' Mrs Enever exclaimed. 'That is such an advantage, isn't it? Just look at the Menemons! When they first appeared I heard people saying, "Shall we receive them?" In no time those very same people were asking, "Will they receive us?" '

'It may be that I am censorious,' the groom's mother continued, expansively. 'It may be, though it is a fault which I try to guard against. But I am not precipitate, and that, I fear, Paul is. You will not believe me when I tell you that he has not known his wife eight weeks.'

'Gracious! I thought they had made mud pies together. Perhaps they will. Matrimony, don't you think, is just full of adventure?'

'And I need not tell you,' Mrs Usher added, 'how grateful I am to the dispensation of Providence which, in putting me in mourning, relieved me of asking people here today. So, while there is that for which I am thankful, there is also that which perturbs. Do you not agree with me, Mr Jones?'

'Entirely, Mrs Usher. Every silver lining has its cloud.' The novelist was about to add further novelties, but Marie beckoned to him. He crossed the room.

'Where is Paul?' the girl asked.

'Playing billiards with your father, I fancy. In Latin countries it is customary for a bride to be taken aside by her mother. Here it is becoming fashionable for a father to disappear with the groom. But don't let it worry you. Disappearances are deceptive.'

In the doorway the butler loomed.

'Harris,' the bride called, 'is the carriage here? Fetch me a cup of bouillon.' She turned to the others. 'It is after 1. The ship sails at 2. But you will all stop and lunch with my father, won't you? Mr. Jones, would you mind very much telling Paul that the carriage is here?'

'It is so unusual,' said Mrs Usher mère, 'for young people to sail for the tropics on their wedding day. Does it not seem unusual to you, also, dear Mrs Metuchen?'

'Gracious!' Mrs Enever exclaimed. 'When I was married I took my husband to Iceland.'

The butler reappeared, preceding a footman who carried a tray, on which there were little cups.

Marie took one. So also did the dowager. As the servants were leaving, Jones, followed by Usher, reëntered the room.

'Before we go, Paul, don't you want some bouillon?' Marie asked.

But either he did not hear or else he did not heed. 'Mother,' he said, 'bring Mrs Enever and come.'

Mrs Usher, who was drinking, lowered her cup. 'We are to lunch here after you and Marie are gone.'

'Marie and I are not going anywhere.'

As he spoke he looked at his bride, and as he looked the cup which she held fell from her hand, spilling over her dress, and then to the floor, where it broke, musically, after the fashion of Sèvres.

Her eyes followed it meditatively. When, presently, she lifted them, the front door had opened and closed. Usher had gone.

'What is the meaning of this?' demanded the dowager. She turned to Mrs Metuchen, from her to Mrs Enever, then to Jones.

'What is the meaning of this?' she repeated. This time she addressed the girl.

Marie nodded, tried to smile, tried, perhaps, to

speak. The effort, though, must have been too great. She dropped forward on her face.

Mrs Metuchen made a dive at the girl. But almost immediately the latter straightened herself.

From without there came a ring.

'Gracious!' exclaimed Mrs Enever. 'It is like a scene in a play.'

Jones blinked appreciatively. 'It is better. This is real drama in real life.'

'But, gracious! what do you suppose ——?'

Jones, however, had no time to waste on Mrs Enever. The groom's mother, with the air of a Gorgon, was promenading toward the door. She seemed smitten by that disease which pathology catalogues as noli me tangere. Her eyes were open to their widest extent, her mouth shut very tight. But Jones was not afraid.

'You'd best wait a moment, Mrs Usher; there is a newspaper man in the hall.'

But the lady herself was not afraid. Her promenade across the room continued, rigidly, almost mechanically, perhaps pleasurably. In a moment she, too, had gone.

Jones turned to the bride. Apparently now she had wholly recovered. She looked precisely as she had five minutes before, as pretty as she could stick, a Venus in her teens. Mrs Metuchen, talking as though the tongue would fall from her mouth, was standing on one side of her. Mrs Enever, doing her best to get a word in edgewise, was standing on the other. Though the one was old and the other young, conjointly they set her off.

Jones was not permitted to stare at her undisturbed. Enever had him by the arm.

'If you love Mammon and abhor righteousness,' the latter was muttering, 'and even if you don't,' he interrupted himself to add, 'tell me what all this mystery is about.'

There are men who can't say, 'I don't know.' It sounds too flat. Jones was one of them. Pontifically, in his deepest note, he replied, 'Mystery, dear boy, exists only in the dictionary. There is no such thing. But there is ignorance, and that is very fertile. The less we know the more we believe. Now, if you want a guess ——' and drawing Enever nearer he whispered in his ear.

Enever shook him off. 'Nonsense!' he sputtered.

'Well, perhaps,' Jones, with silken sweetness, answered, 'perhaps it is nonsense; but then, you see, we have been exchanging ideas.'

The shot might have told, yet it lacked the time. Before it could hit, there was Mr Mermex.

'Archibald,' chuckled Mrs Metuchen, 'look at your work! You have killed your daughter, you ——'

Marie interrupted her. She had risen. 'You might better have stayed in Frisco, I think. Don't you?' she added, longly. As she spoke, she smiled. 'And just look at my dress! I am dripping with soup.'

Brushing her father aside, leisurely, without haste, smiling still, she crossed the room and left it.

'There goes a dream in lilac,' Jones confided to Enever.

'One from which Usher appears to have awakened.'

'The more fool he, then.'

Enever had no chance to reply. His wife sailed up to him and sailed him away.

Mrs Metuchen had evaporated. Jones and Mr Mermex were alone.

The latter coughed. 'You are a literary man, I believe?'

'Oh, no. I write little things for the magazines. There is nothing literary in that.'

To this Mr Mermex assented, but absently. It was evident that he was sparring for wind. 'At least, you are a friend of these people, a friend also of my daughter; and here I have few. Will you give me a moment?'

'The plot thickens,' Jones reflected. 'He is going to use me for a sewer.'

'Now,' Mr Mermex continued, 'when you met my

daughter last summer, did it occur to you to ask her where she had been?'

'But, my dear sir, a man of sense never asks a lady where she has been. He asks where she is going.'

'No doubt. Even otherwise Marie would not have told. Explanations are not her weakness. But that is a detail. She had just left Sioux Falls.'

'Ah!' In the rug which Jones had been studying abruptly understanding dawned. An entire panorama unrolled — the cat, the bag, the key to the whole situation. 'Was that what you told Usher?' he asked.

Mr Mermex nodded.

'But permit me, why, of all other moments, did you choose the one which you took?'

'Why, indeed! I had to take what I could get. I only reached here an hour ago.'

'Of course. Then, too, postage is dear and tele-graphing expensive; yet I can't help thinking, since the matter appears to have weighed on your con-science, that a little extravagance ——'

The father coughed again. 'There is the point. Marie wrote me that she was to marry Usher. I wrote her to go ahead. On the train this morning I met the beast from whom I thought she was free. He told me that he had never been served, that the divorce was invalid, that he intended to rip it up — all of which I had to tell Usher, and when I did, you saw what occurred. He reasoned, I suppose, that if Number One got at him he would be in for damages, and heavy ones, too. Don't you think so?'

'Really, the processes of Usher's reasoning exceed my powers of imagination. If your supposition be correct, certainly his commercial instinct is beautifully developed. But personally I regard it as a great mistake to neglect pleasure for business.'

'Now,' said Mr Mermex, 'there is a reporter out there. What shall I say to him? There is no use keeping him waiting.'

'None at all. Particularly as in all probability he enjoys it. Tell him the reverse. Tell him it is a great mistake to neglect business for pleasure.'

'Quite so.'

The doorbell rang again.

'There is another of them, I suppose, and that reminds me, you will stop, won't you, and have lunch with us?'

'No, thanks very much; but you might say to your daughter, with my compliments, that divorce is the mother-in-law of invention, and that I wish her again many happy returns.'

'You are very thoughtful of others,' a lady in lilac called from the adjoining room, 'yet in the circumstances a trifle cynical, too.'

Jones picked up his hat. 'I dare say, but then, you

see, it is in thoughtfulness of others that cynicism begins.'

'Yes, indeed,' said a voice from the doorway, 'let us think of ourselves. There,' Usher continued, as he entered where they stood, 'I have been off reconnoitering. The divorce is all right. The forces centripetal and centrifugal couldn't touch it. Marie, where are you?'

From the adjoining room the bride strolled — a festival of beauty in the festival of life.

With a look cannibalistic in its longing to eat her, Usher added, 'My dear, we have lost the boat.'

The girl's moist lips, parting in a smile, disclosed the point of her tongue. 'Then can't we,' she inquired, with an air of innocence which was simply seraphic, 'can't we manage to find a train?'

'Any port in a honeymoon,' Usher answered. 'Let's be off at once.'

'My blessing on you both,' cried Mr Mermex.

' 'Twas ever thus,' said Jones. 'Woman proposes and a poor devil accepts. For such is the noose matrimonial.'

*A Drama in a
Drawing Room*

A Drama
in a Drawing Room

IN the multiple brilliancies of the dining-room I found myself at the left of the Duchess Sally. Ever since her girlhood I had known her. At Narragansett Pier, in the good old nights before the Casino was dreamed of, I had sat with her on verandas that were vibrant with osculations. That was some time ago. Her subsequent transatlantic triumphs and spectacular marriage to the Duc de Malakoff are now ancient and familiar history — so ancient even that I am dispensed from noting that Sally is no chicken. But though her youth had gone, her heart is young. Hence, no doubt, in disregard of every canon of precedence, my place beside her. But then, as I have intimated, she never was ceremonious.

Across the glittering service, beyond the gold branches of the lusters, sat Monsieur de Malakoff. Between him and Sally there were, including myself, fourteen other people. Over the bisque I had taken them in. Barring a nuncio and an aunt of Sally —

Mrs Nicholas Manhattan — I knew none of them. Barring two others, the rest of the party interested me but mediocrally. Of these two one was a vision in white, a delicious apparition that suggested the pays des songes; a face infinitely delicate and of exceeding beauty. The other was a young man who looked as the musketeer Aramis might in modern dress. His features were chiseled. On his lip was a mustache that seemingly had been drawn with a crayon. His hair was black, slightly curled; his eyes were Polar blue, and their lashes long as a girl's. I should have thought him too good-looking for a man had it not been for his chin, which was resolute, and the expression of his mouth, which was as firm and as chill as steel. Next to him was the vision. They were talking inaudibly together.

The bisque had gone. The maître d'hôtel, followed by valets de pied, was presenting sturgeon from the Volga. Turning to Sally I asked who the young man was.

'The Marquis de Parabole,' she answered. 'That is his wife, next to you.' Sally would have said more, perhaps, but the nuncio was claiming her attention.

Already I had noticed my neighbor, a little, red-headed woman, who, in face and manner, suggested a bird — yet, perhaps, a bird of prey. In any event, a bird that, with beak and talons, knows how to defend its own. In the word or two that I had already exchanged with her I knew by her accent that she could not be French, or, for that matter, Anglo-Saxon.

Presently our earlier conversation was resumed. At some remark of mine she smiled. I have never forgotten that smile. It disclosed a front tooth filled with a diamond.

The effect was startling and at the same time evocative. I recalled that the arrangement was affectioned in certain sections of South America, and it occurred to me that the lady might be a Brazilian — a supposition which subsequent developments confirmed. Yet that which at the time intrigued me most was her relationship to the young musketeer. I could have sworn that she would never see 40 again, and that he was yet to see 29. It seemed to me that I must have misunderstood Sally. But a look, which, in a pause of our talk, she shot across the table, undeceived me. It was double-barreled and aimed point-blank at the musketeer and the vision. There was hatred in it. Had I not already likened the lady to a bird I should add that there was venom in it, too. Could a look kill, there would have been murder then and there. A moment and it had gone. Her beady eyes shifted to mine.

A filet of reindeer was being served. From beyond

came the rich voice of Monsieur de Malakoff. He appeared to be philosophizing on the degree of decomposition that renders game most savorous. Meanwhile, in the constant replenishment of blond wines, conversation and the tone of it heightened. The young musketeer was still talking inaudibly with that vision, but otherwise the table was united. Topics were tossed like balls. Jests flared as pinwheels do. Wit, or at least a passable imitation of it, became common property, until, in a ripple of laughter created by a suggestion only a trifle more scabreux than the last, Sally arose, and from the gayety of the room we passed into others yet gayer.

It was not for the sake of gayety that I was then in Paris. On the contrary, I was at work on a history of the young empresses of old Rome. For such labors there is nothing more serviceable than the Bibliothèque Nationale. Hence the sojourn.

The morning succeeding the dinner I went as usual to the Library. The documents that I there obtained held certain stupefactions; but my surprise at what I read was exceeded by my surprise at what I saw. At a table beyond was the young musketeer. Fancy a panther in a conservatory! Yet there he sat, fronted by a pile of MSS., and as lost in them as presently I became in the Subura. When I emerged from that Whitechapel of the past, he saw me and smiled in recognition.

A few days later at the Café Anglais, where, because of its proximity to the Library, I was in the habit of lunching, we met again, and in meeting, joined tables. For a while conversation drifted impersonally, but presently the moi popped out.

'May I, without indiscretion,' I asked, 'inquire the nature of your distractions at the Bibliothèque?'

'Alchemy,' he answered. 'But,' he added, with a smile in which there was amusement at my manifest surprise, 'let me ask what are your distractions there.'

'Nothing half so fascinating,' I replied. 'I am merely a writer.'

'In that case,' he retorted, 'you are an alchemist, too. A wad of paper and an ounce of ink you transform into bank notes. The transmutation of metals is a process only a trifle more elaborate. Others have practiced it successfully, and what has been done may be repeated.'

'No doubt,' I answered; 'but the age of miracles has gone.'

'Has it?' he asked, with an air of great innocence. 'That, really, I did not know. I fancied that it had come. I believe that could the people who lived in what you call the age of miracles return they would be far more astonished at contemporary wonders

than we are at those of the past. Tenez, monsieur.
Just across the river is the Église de Ste. Chose. Its
construction must have cost a lot, yet it was built by
a poor devil of a bookseller who emerged from grind-
ing poverty into abnormal wealth — relatively speaking, that is, for in his time even the richest were none
too well off. For that matter, they are none too well
off now. It is in wealth alone that the world has not
progressed. Kings today have to count the pennies.
Budgets are out at elbows. France, the most opulent
country in Europe, is obliged to consider penuriously
the cost of an ironclad. In early times there was
nothing of this. The kings that were built at will
cities of enchanted dwellings, shimmering avenues,
and walls so wide that they were race courses. The
treasures that Alexander looted provided him with
coin to the value of fifteen billion francs, a sum
tolerably large, and yet paltry beside the four hundred and twenty-five billion that is estimated to have
been the value of the treasure heaped on the pile of
Assurbanipal.

'Whence did wealth in such proportions come?
Through what wizardry were the fairylands that existed then created? Obviously, there was a secret,
and that secret has been lost. At the beginning of the
present era the total amount of money in circulation
was a hundred times inferior to that which in earlier

days a single satrap possessed. Thereafter the world
grew steadily poorer. It was not until after the dis-
covery of the Americas that wealth began to look up.
But what are the world's riches now in comparison to
what they were? There was not only a secret, and a
secret that has been lost, but that secret was the
transmutation of metals. Its fading memories used to
haunt the minds of men. The attempts of Caligula to
regain them are historic. They hallucinated the
Middle Ages. Geber's theory, that metals are compound bodies made up of mercury and sulphur in
different proportions, fascinated every alchemist,
even to Roger Bacon, for he, too, had crucibles, alem-
bics, and aludels at work. In Paracelsus the effort
culminated. He demonstrated that there is an un-
known element, a quintessence, which he called the
alcahest, and which when recovered would do the
trick. That quintessence, Flamel, the bookseller
whom I mentioned, found. I was going over one of
his manuscripts today. There, monsieur ——'

For a moment he fumbled in his pocket. Then he
drew out an envelope, which he handed me. On it
were signs quite cabalistic and figures equally ab-
struse. Yet from it there emanated an odor of orris,
and I could not but notice that it was addressed to
the marquis at a club. It naturally occurred to me
that in addition to the distractions that he admitted

he probably had others that he concealed. I am not censorious, and in view of the lady with the diamond tooth, I did not blame him in the least.

'There,' he resumed, 'are the component parts. I jotted them on that envelope,' he interrupted himself to explain, 'because it was the only bit of paper I had. But that is the formula.'

With that he ran on into technical terms, which conveyed no meaning to me, and my attention wandered until arrested by an entirely intelligible mention of flesh and blood.

'Human?' I asked, with pardonable surprise.

'Yes,' he answered, 'that is best. But nowadays people have such prejudices. Yet there is the alcahest.'

He paused, glanced at the envelope, from it to me, and then, with that grace of manner which only Latins have, apologized for the dissertation. 'Anything theoretical is so tiresome,' he added, in his winning way. 'Yet if by chance the subject has the merit of interesting you, I should be glad if you would accompany me to my shop. My home,' he continued, 'is in the Avenue Marceau, but for this work I have a maisonnette in the Rue de la Pompe, which I fitted up expressly. There I could have the pleasure of showing you an experiment or two.'

The stupefactions of the Subura claimed me still.

I had counted on a long afternoon at the Library. I was stupid enough to prefer the society of a dead empress to a living alchemist, and I thanked him. Whereupon, after paying our scores — scores that included strawberries at a franc apiece, which, I mind me now, were fully worth it — we got out into the sunshine and absinthe of the street, where, little dreaming in what dramatic circumstances I was to see him again, we parted.

The dead empress detained me in Paris until, ejected by the heat, I ran down to Etretat. There, at the Casino one noon when looking over The Figaro, I jumped as though a dog had bitten me. I think any one else might have done so, too. I had happened on the account — with which all the world has since been familiar — of the arrest of the Marquis de Parabole for murder.

On the esplanade without was the usual throng of people that gathers there during the hour that precedes the déjeuner and succeeds the dip. Among them was my old friend, Mrs Manhattan. Thinking that I might furnish a fillip for her breakfast, I approached her.

I have sometimes thought that horrors appeal to women more than they do to men. I am often in error; I may have been then, yet, as I greeted this lady, it seemed to me that she was reveling in the revelations. It is true that she knew De Parabole, and acquaintance with people lends an admitted charm to anything that you may read about them. The worse it is the better you like it. Mrs Manhattan was radiant. From the manner in which she spoke it seemed to me that nothing had pleased her more since the day the news reached her of Sally's engagement. I presumed to say as much, but she turned on me quite viciously.

'When a man kills his wife ——' she began.

'His wife!' I exclaimed. 'The Figaro did not say that.'

'Bother The Figaro! It was his wife he killed. First he took her money, now he takes her life. If a man marries a Hottentot, then, Hottentot though she be, he ought to treat her decently, instead of which, after making her life a curse, he boils her up in a cauldron.'

'Nonsense!' I threw in. 'Besides, she isn't a Hottentot; she is a Brazilian.'

'It is quite the same to me,' Mrs Manhattan, with superb indifference to ethnology, threw back. 'He ought to be drawn and quartered. In my presence once he contradicted her flatly.'

'Yes, that is just it,' I managed to remark. 'A woman will act on a man's nerves day in, day out, and if, under constant fire, his nerves once give way and he calls his soul his own, he is nothing more or less than a brute.'

'That's right,' Mrs Manhattan, with great irony, retorted; 'that's right. Justify him entirely. A man who murders his wife ought to decorated. I know all that. I have heard it before. But only in France. And since in France you feel as Frenchmen do, I can't see why you don't run up and congratulate him.'

Abashed and hushed, I had no recourse but to retreat. When, a few weeks later, I reached Paris, the preliminary examination had been concluded and the trial was announced. At that trial I determined to be present. Others did, too. So many, in fact, that but a fraction got in. But journalism is a sesame. As a member of the press I succeeded where members of Parliament failed. I not only succeeded in getting in, I succeeded in getting a seat — a stall, rather. In the interrogatory that ensued a drama unrolled.

For setting, there were bare white walls, which a crucifix dominated. Fronting the audience was the tribunal. There, robed in red, the president and the assessors sat. Before them was a display of exhibits. To the left was the jury. In the dock, to the right, was the prisoner. As I seated myself he looked over at me and smiled, very much as he had in the

Library. He seemed as out of place in the Cour d'Assises as he had in the Bibliothèque Nationale. There he had suggested a panther in a conservatory, here a prince in the galleys; and I could not but marvel at the intricacies of the mystery we call life, which had led him from one to the other.

These meditations a greffier interrupted. The indictment was being read. At its conclusion the president turned to the prisoner.

'What have you to say, De Parabole?'

'That you wish my head, monsieur,' the marquis answered, as he arose. 'I regret to be unwilling to oblige you with it.'

The president pursed his lips and surveyed the court. 'That is natural,' he answered, at last. 'But for the moment it is beside the issue. Where were you on the night of the 12th of July?'

'That question I have already refused to answer.'

The president pursed his lips again. He reminded me of nothing so much as a salamander. His mouth had the same width and his chin the same recession.

'Yes, I am aware of it,' he continued. 'You left the juge d'instruction to infer that you were occupied with some gallant adventure. For the moment we will let that go, too. Meanwhile, you may tell me the object of your separate establishment in the Rue de la Pompe.'

'Experimental researches.'

'That, I am also aware, is your defense. It is not unadroit. It explains the presence there of an arsenal of chemicals. But it does not explain the presence of other things concerning which you shall have an opportunity of enlightening the jury. You have frequently quarreled with the deceased.'

'If,' the marquis answered, 'you refer to Madame De Parabole, I do not know that she is dead. Nor,' he added, with entire courtesy, 'do you.'

'I at least know that she is not to be found. The prosecution has searched for her everywhere. But the search was not otherwise fruitless. It has been discovered that at the time of your marriage you had nothing but your title. Your wife, previously a widow, was the daughter of a rich Brazilian. Her property you dissipated. That accomplished, you again had nothing but your title. With a view to bartering it anew you devise an elaborate scheme. You give out that you are an alchemist. You fit up a laboratory. You stock it with chemicals. On the evening of July 12th you lure your wife there. She drives up to the door in her carriage, dismisses it, and enters the house. She has never been seen since that moment. But later that evening a passer hears a scream. At midnight another passer notices a reflection of flame. What were you doing at that hour?'

'I have forgotten.'

'Very good. I will tell you. You were destroying the remains of your wife whom you had murdered. But you did not destroy them entirely. In a cauldron in that den of yours were discovered, together with bits of bone, some thick, brown ooze in which were traces of caustic soda and caustic potash. Experts will demonstrate that by means of these chemicals a human body can be converted into just such ooze. Do you deny it?'

'On the contrary, it is quite true. Only in this instance it happens that the ooze was the residue of the body of a gorilla which I had obtained from the Jardin d'Acclimatation.'

'That defense you advanced before the juge d'instruction. Inquiries made of the management show that you did acquire a gorilla. But it was only a part of this plot of yours. It was only that, in case of misadventure, you might have a ready answer. In any event, the gorilla obtained by you did not, I suppose, have a tooth filled with a diamond. A tooth set with a diamond was found in that ooze. A tooth filled with a diamond was the peculiar characteristic of the deceased. Here it is. I invite you to be seated.'

'Silence!'

The courtroom, suddenly murmurous with indignation, hummed like a wasp's nest. I could see men gesticulating. A woman fainted.

'Silence!' a crier repeated.

The prisoner seemed unmoved. A fat man approached and addressed him. I heard some one say that it was Maître Dupin, his advocate.

The president, who had reminded me of a salamander, looked now like a wolf; but a wolf that has fed. Turning to a huissier, he ordered him to call the first witness, and presently the coachman who, on the night of the 12th of July, had driven the marquise to the Rue de la Pompe was testifying to that effect. He was succeeded by other witnesses — by agents and experts, who corroborated the president's arraignment. When they had gone the avocat général addressed the jury, summing up the evidence, deducing from it the guilt of the accused, clearly, logically, without oratory or literature.

'Any question of mitigating circumstances,' he concluded, 'is out of place in a case such as this. Yet if your conscience hesitates, it is your duty to acquit that man. But if you are absolutely convinced that he is an assassin, it is equally your duty to declare him guilty. I have no wish to say that the blood of his victim cries for vengeance. Of vengeance I know nothing. What I demand of you is justice.'

'Silence!' the crier repeated.

Again the room was humming like a wasp's nest. But this time it was murmurous with applause. In the subsidence of that applause the fat man stood up. In his hand he held a paper, at which he glanced. Then he bowed, first to the bench, afterward to the jury.

'Gentlemen,' he began, 'it had been my intention when I reached here this morning to open my address to you with a citation, not from the code, but from a novel. In the "Affaire Lerouge," the most famous story of the famous Gaboriau, a man is arrested for murder. Against him are advanced proofs quite as convincing as those that have been brought against Monsieur de Parabole. But the magistrate having asked him where he was during the night of the crime, and he having refused to reply, the magistrate cried: "Release him; he has no alibi, he is innocent." Gentlemen, after reminding you of that subtle and, as it was subsequently shown, correct deduction, it had been my intention to demonstrate to you that the essence of crime is the motive, and that here none has been shown. It had also been my intention to display to you my client in his true light, a young seigneur who, through unfortunate speculations at the Bourse, had lost, not merely his wife's fortune, but his own, and who was seeking to recover both through the transmutation of metals. Whether such transmutation be possible, whether or not — as Monsieur de Parabole had confided to me — he was on the point of recovering that solvent which is alleged to have existed, I am not competent to affirm. But on entering here this morning I did feel competent to use the exhibits that are piled on this table, and to show from them that whether or not the pursuits of Monsieur de Parabole were chimerical, at least they were not criminal. Among those exhibits but one object embarrassed me. That object is the diamond tooth. Even with my client's aid and my best endeavors I felt unable to explain its presence by any theory of coincidences that would have been satisfactory, but it had been my intention to leave it to you to decide whether a man should lose his head because some one else had lost a tooth. These demonstrations that I was prepared to set before you I am now dispensed from elaborating. I let them go, vaguely outlined as they are, for, gentlemen, the Marquise de Parabole is dead indeed, only she did not die in the Rue de la Pompe, she did not die on the 12th of July. She died the day before yesterday in Rio de Janeiro!'

'Silence in this court!' It was the president who was commanding quiet now. There was no longer a murmur, there was a tumult, in which the whole vast room had joined.

'Silence!' he commanded again. Then, turning to Maître Dupin, 'What evidence,' he asked, 'have you in support of this statement?'

'A cablegram brought to me half an hour ago, which I shall have the honor of submitting to you. Dated Rio, it is addressed to Dr Rosa e Silva, the Brazilian Consul here, and it states that Madame de Parabole died there, as I have represented, the day before yesterday, twenty-four hours after landing. I am aware, monsieur le président, that it will have to be verified, but meanwhile I ask that the trial be adjourned.'

Mopping his fat face, Maître Dupin bowed and sat down. I could have embraced him. I wanted to tell him so. But the avocat général was speaking now.

'The obvious good faith and high professional standing of the gentleman for the defense relieve me,' he was saying, 'from opposing his suggestion. Yet I must admit ——'

What he was about to admit no one heeded. The salle was again in commotion. Everybody was talking at once. At the moment I could not see the prisoner. Maître Dupin was bending over him, and presently, through the tumult, circulating above and accentuating it, mounted the shrill call of the crier. Then I became conscious that I had assisted at a coup de théâtre which, for sheer poignancy, I had

never seen equaled on the stage, and, precisely as
from a play, I found myself drifting out with the
crowd to the street.

It was months later, in the multiple brilliancies of
the Malakoff dining-room, that the last act was
given. Meanwhile I had gone to New York and returned. It was June again; and again, in defiance of
every canon of precedence, I was seated at Sally's
left. Across the table was the young musketeer, and
across the table, too, was the delicious vision. On
the other side of me was Mrs Manhattan. From beyond, through the gold branches of the lusters, came
the rich voice of the duke. He was philosophizing,
as a great noble may, on the superiority of white
truffles over black. In appreciating the fine discrim-
ination I could not but reflect that his ancestor, the
Napoleonic hero, who had won a duchy with a sword,
would have appreciated it still more. These reflections Mrs Manhattan interrupted.

'There is a subject for you. Why not write it up?'

'Monsieur de Malakoff's physiology of taste?' I
asked.

'No; Monsieur de Parabole's physiology of marriage. You know, do you not, that he is engaged to
——' and Mrs Manhattan, with a quiver of the eye-
lids, indicated the delicious vision. 'That is what
killed the Hottentot. The poor old thing knew what

was going on. A man may betray the woman who loves him, but never can he deceive her.'

'Quite so,' I answered; 'and it was by way of love-token, I suppose, that she extracted that ornament from her mouth and left it where the police could make the worst of it. When I read in the papers that this lady had first planted her tooth and then vanished in order that he might be guillotined for her murder, mentally I took off my hat to the medievalism of her imagination. But though I took off my hat, were I De Parabole I would have taken her life had she not conveniently died in the interim.'

'Oh, yes,' Mrs Manhattan returned, with a suggestion of sarcasm, which at the moment escaped me. 'You, of course, would have done wonders.'

'But I must ask him,' I continued, 'whether or not he is still in search of the alcahest.'

'The what? The alcahest? What is that?'

'A synonym for happiness,' I explained. Then after glancing at some blond wine that a footman was serving I looked over at the delicious vision.

'And happiness, to my thinking,' I added, 'consists, if it consists in anything, in the kiss of one girl.'

But my views were unnoticed. Sally was rising, and from the brilliancies of the dining-room we passed to other rooms yet more brilliant.

The Top of the Heap

The Top of the Heap

B LIND obedience and the truth. That's what
I want from you. Nothing else.'

Mr Beamish, as he spoke, glared imperially.
There are men whom it is more agreeable to avoid
than to meet. Mr Beamish had succeeded in becoming one of them. He was fat, and quite as fascinating
as vulgarity and a French tailor could make him.
What a French tailor can accomplish in that line ex-
ceeds the powers of prose. Yet, though fat, he was
forceful, and if vulgar, valiant.

It was his son whom he addressed. The room,
large, oblong, furnished in red, tropically hot on this
mid-May noon, had the tawdriness of a Paris hotel
written all over it. Through an open window the sun
lurched. Beyond were the Tuileries. From below
came the cries of the hawkers that are never still,
'Le Matin! Demandez Le Matin!'

'Now disobey me if you dare ——'

The boy made a face. He was rather good looking,
and quite athletic.

'Disobey you! Disobey a father who is a pheno-

menon, a father with thirty million and three chins!
What do you take me for? But how do you know
she won't object?'

'Because she does what her mamma wishes.'

'But I don't see why her mamma should wish anything of the kind, or, for that matter, you either.'

'You don't, eh? I am decently fixed, am I not? I
did the fixing myself, didn't I? What did I do it
for? Why do you suppose that after mining in Mon-
tana I monkeyed with Morgan, rolled Rockefeller,
and got ahead of Gates? For the fun of it? There is
no fun in a job like that. To donate libraries? That
is Carnegie's patent. I want to splurge. In that new
house of mine on Fifth Avenue I want to give cotillons and dinner dances — cotillons with automobiles
and Russian sables for favors, dinner dances with
government bonds for boutonnières. I want to be
top of the heap.'

'Noble ambition.'

'And why not? Supposing I am self-made. I am as
rich as Crœsus, whoever he may be, and just as good
as the rest of them. The trouble is that in New York
I don't know anybody — except from 10 to 3. Out of
Wall Street I am seven-eighths offered and nothing
bid. But here it is different. On this side people who
have position don't seem to be as much afraid of

losing it as they are at home. You have noticed that
yourself, haven't you?'

The young man yawned and nodded.

'Anyway,' Mr Beamish resumed, 'that's been the
case with the Finsburys. They are bankrupt, it is
true, but they are not bounders, and provided I produce enough they are willing that you should marry
their daughter and take her back to New York.
There all you will have to do is to fill my house with
the smart set. And they'll come, too; they'll come on
a run when they find a duke's daughter is there to
receive them.'

'But what if I don't like the girl?'

Mr Beamish stood up and reached for a hat. 'You
have got to like her,' he answered shortly. 'Come.
It's time for business. Ring the bell, and see if the
auto is ready.'

The auto was. And presently, after a series of
touf-toufs, a whizz up the Champs Elysées, a bolt
into the Avenue Marceau, father and son were let
into the drawing-room of an appartement meublé, a
miniature salon, cream and gold, and tenderly pink,
where loomed a dowager, robust and rancid, flanking
a tall, large-mouthed, small-eyed girl.

'Duchess, this is my son Harry,' Mr Beamish began, and, plucking at his collar, and finding it moist,
mopped himself abundantly.

The duchess assumed an expression of great amiability. 'My daughter, the Lady Angelica,' she announced, with a wave of her fan, and with another, she added: 'I am so sorry Finsbury is not in. But he has a perfect mania for going to the dentist's, and that, I think, shows so much conscientiousness. Do sit down.'

The girl had moved to a sofa. Harry took a seat at her side. Mr Beamish and the duchess ranged themselves opposite.

'Warm day,' said the fat man. At once he and his hostess lost themselves in cognate reflections.

'Do you like Paris?' Harry asked of the girl, who just raised her eyes to his. 'I prefer London. But New York is good enough for me. You have never been there, have you?'

The Lady Angelica flushed, her eyes flickered, her lips half parted, then, as though by a sheer effort of will, her mouth shut tight. What she meant by the mummery Harry could not tell. But he took it for British reserve.

'Yes,' Harry continued, indifferently, 'New York is a mighty nice place. We make a specialty of tall houses, high winds, beautiful manners, ready-made clothes, and pretty girls. It is all due to the climate, I believe. Did I understand you to say that you had been there?'

'My daughter,' the duchess overloudly interrupted, 'has not traveled much; she ——'

Harry turned. His father was contemplating a Cupid on the ceiling. The duchess seemed to have one eye on him, the other on Angelica.

'She is only recently out of the schoolroom, you know, and —— Come here, Posey!'

Suddenly from somewhere, presumably from under the sofa, there filtered the cry of a cat.

'Come here, Posey, Posey, Posey.' And the duchess, leaning forward, snapped her fingers enticingly.

Mr Beamish stood up. Harry also was rising; the girl, too. Previously flushed; now she was pale.

'They seem to have forgotten to give poor little Posey his breakfast,' the duchess added, in smiling explanation. 'But you are not going, are you? Finsbury will be so sorry. Yet, why not dine with us tomorrow, just a plain family dinner at 8, and afterward my little girl can show you her water colors. She fairly dotes on water colors, and that, I think, shows such a pure mind.'

'Tomorrow, I am afraid,' Harry interjected, but his father managed to kick him.

'He will be proud to come. But how about today? Couldn't you both lunch with us at Paillard's? My auto can take you there and back in a jiffy.'

'That is my brother's stepdaughter,' the duchess remarked to Harry, who was examining a photograph on the mantel. 'Do you think she resembles Lady Essex? So many do.'

Harry moved closer to the picture. The duchess seized the opportunity to whisper to Mr. Beamish behind her fan. In a moment Harry turned.

'We shall love to,' the duchess resumed. 'Lunching at Paillard's will be quite an escapade. But we shan't trouble you to bring us back. Our brougham can fetch us. And you won't mind waiting a moment, while we put on our hats? Angelica!'

Trailing her daughter behind her, the duchess sailed from the room. Father and son were alone.

'Nice girl,' Mr. Beamish remarked, as the door closed.

'A peach. And so chatty.'

'Now see that you make up to her at luncheon. There is nothing like catching a girl on the fly.'

'Give me a hundred thousand a year, and catch her yourself, then. Matrimony, with a pretty girl at the other end, must be jolly good fun. But with her! Cæsar's ghost! It would be medicine. That's the truth.'

'It is, is it? Well, I want obedience also. You may take your medicine or your walking-stick. Just say which, and be quick.'

Harry glared about the room.   Through its cream,
and   gold,   and   tender   pink,   the   future   surged.
Divested of its garland of millions that future looked
quite bleak.

Mr. Beamish stamped a foot.

'Which?'

'Medicine,' the boy answered, savagely. 'I'll be
shot, though, if I don't take it in capsules.'

'Don't be slangy,' retorted the plutocrat, in whose
phraseology capsules had no definite meaning.

'Scat!' cried Harry.   'There's that beastly cat
again.'

From beyond there filtered anew a shrill meow.
But immediately a door opened. The duchess, trailing her daughter, reappeared, and, presently, during
an interchange of uplifting intellectualities, the street
was reached, the auto hummed into the Champs
Elysées, bowled down the avenue, and drew up at
Paillard's.

The canopied terrace was filled with people of
manifest distinction, with horizontales and femmes
du monde, exotics and cercleux, diplomats, and
rastas. From a hall adjoining there issued the murmur of harps, the kiss of flutes, the caress of cling-
ing measures. In the air was the savor of pine apples,
the smell of orris, the odor of food and flowers, of
pretty women and smart men, the atmosphere of

what the French call High Life, and pronounce Hig Leaf. Mr Beamish inhaled it voluptuously. Preceded by two maîtres d'hôtel, he led his guests to a table.

'Do you chauffe?' Harry asked Angelica, when all were seated.

'Do you, Mr Harry?' the duchess inquired, in her stead. 'I have not let my little girl learn yet, but she is passionately fond of collecting postage stamps, and that, I think, shows so much adaptability. But automobiling is very jolly, is it not?'

'It beats bridge,' Harry answered. 'Wouldn't you like to learn,' he continued, turning to the girl.

The Lady Angelica could not speak; her mouth was full of melon.

'That is the King of the Belgians,' said the duchess, indicating a voluminously bearded old party, who was being helped to a chair near by. 'And is not that Mr Astor, over there? We used to think,' she continued, expansively, 'that he might marry among us. But his daughter will. Our young men have such a fondness for your pretty compatriots, and that, I think, shows so much entente cordiale. No, Mr Beamish, no champagne; a drop of Eau de Vals if you will. After Paget, and Essex, and Craven and Curzon, then Marlborough, and, recently, Manchester, not to speak of my brother, who married a

New Yorker, a Mrs Morningside, of Morningside
Park, a widow, with a daughter, such a dear, too,
who, I fancy, will marry among us also. You know
my brother, do you not, Mr Beamish? But fair exchange, I often think, is not snobbery; is it, Mr
Harry? And does it not seem to you as though some
of you young Americans should begin now, and lay
siege to our lovely English girls. Thank you, a bit of
the wing, nothing else.'

Harry turned anew to the Lady Angelica. 'How
would you like to be besieged by an American?' he
asked, seductively.

The girl flushed. Apparently, she was about to
reply, but British reserve may have prevented. She
flushed afresh and looked away.

With superior tact the duchess intervened. 'Tell
me, Mr Harry, is not that your ambassador over
there?'

Harry turned. As he did so he heard a little plain-
tive cry. He turned again.

'The large, handsome man near the entrance,' the
duchess insistently continued, and actually pointed
with her fan.

Harry was forced to turn once more. The cry was
repeated, but less plaintively, in a note louder and
more shrill.

Again Harry turned. Others were turning, too.

The King wheeled in his chair. A cocotte near him put her glasses up.

Angelica's face was hid by a fan. Her thin frame shook. She seemed convulsed with laughter, with a churchlike desire to conceal it, too. Mr Beamish was examining his fork as though it were a great curiosity.

In hasty astonishment an omnibus began ferreting under the table. With the same superior tact the duchess waved him away.

'Ce n'est rien,' she announced. 'Une petite Angora, voilà tout. Angelica, you ought not to have brought her. Mr Harry, would you be good enough, that is, my man out there'—as she spoke she motioned at the street—'would you mind fetching him? I will send Posey home by him. Poor, dear, little thing, it is the smell of ris de veau. She just dotes on ris de veau.'

'And that,' said Harry, in open mimic of the duchess, 'shows, I think, such a candid nature.'

He got from his seat and made for the entrance. But in the street he discovered that he must have misunderstood the lady. The man he fancied hers spoke no human tongue. He bothered for a moment or two with another servant, but the latter turned out to be the King's.

Harry started to go back. As he did so, he beheld

the duchess entering a cab that stood a trifle beyond. Angelica was at her heels. Mr Beamish was helping them both.

Harry hurried forward. 'You are not going to take Posey home, are you?' he asked, a hand on the door. 'Why, give her to me. I'll do it myself. Where is she?'

He looked from mother to daughter. Both were seated now. The girl had her veil down, but through it, at the question, he could see her mouth contract, then it opened, and from it issued a distinct meow.

Mr Beamish slammed the door. 'Allez', he bellowed.

Quite flabbergasted, Harry fell back. His astonishment was not unnatural. Not until that moment had it occurred to him that the cat and the girl were one. Then, also, he had never heard a girl meow before. Yet, girls have, and will. Not often, of course, but semi-occasionally, in certain clinics — which Harry had never visited — and in certain treatises — which he had never read. To this inexperience and illiteracy his surprise was due.

'So — so, that is Posey?' he stuttered. 'So that is Posey, is it?' he repeated instantly, in a voice more assured. 'Well, you may marry that tomcat yourself. For I shan't,' he added, defiantly. 'Not for a million a month. Not for the top of the heap.'

But he addressed the Champs Elysées. His words were lost in the roar of the wide, white street. Mr Beamish had swung into an automobile, and, in derision, perhaps, was touf-toufing away.

The machine floated on and up toward the Arc, through the glittering haze, through the swarm of glittering traps. Harry watched it go. As it fled a fantasy of finance, felines, and felonies formed and fluttered before him.

Then suddenly the vision of plutocracy and caterwauls faded away. A diminutive groom, impertinent yet correct, had, from the box of a brougham, swung, an inch from his toes. But it was not the boy, nor yet the brougham, nor even an obese coachman, who held the reins, that had vaporized his thoughts. Within the carriage a girl sat staring straight into his face.

As his eyes mingled with her own she turned. He could see her profile. He could see, too, that he had seen it before. But where? In dream? In the Louvre? In the picture of Psyche made by Gérard? Neither the lady or her tiger gave him time to determine. A door was being opened, and she was stepping out.

Then, in the perfection of the ravishment of a frock such as perhaps Doucet alone in all the world can produce, he beheld a waist that would fit in a garter, the figure of a willis in a ballad, the incandescence of beauty beautifully bedraped.

But what was she saying? Was it language of Olympus, or the tongue of France, in which she was deigning to address the groom? Yet manifestly the latter understood. He was tipping his hat. And immediately, too, Harry was enlightened. In those accents which certain sections of Fifth Avenue share with Mayfair there fell from lips of silk the perfectly plain and entirely intelligible Anglo-Saxon order: 'Follow me.'

At once, under the chaperonage of the brougham, of the enormous coachman and diminutive groom, up the wide avenue she strolled.

The majority of women walk badly. It was a pleasure to watch this young person, and that pleasure Harry proceeded to enjoy. When she had stepped from the carriage, he had enveloped her with that look which strips from neck to knee. But she had not condescended to notice it, and now, her head erect, her nose in the air, her body unswayed, she passed along, disdainful, indifferent, and serene.

These airs affected him but mediocrally. It occurred to him that she was probably taking that promenade which succeeds the morning canter, and precedes the divertissements of the five o'clock, and in those divertissements he determined to participate.

How he was to manage it he did not bother himself to ask. Once he passed her, but, of course, she did not look his way. He dropped behind, yet in the dropping there was not so much as the quiver of an eyelid to betoken a consciousness of his impertinence.

Women admire the brave when they do not prefer the audacious. Harry recognized the beauty of the truth of that axiom, even though he omitted to formulate it. He wanted to be devilish. He longed to. Yet how, barring downright caddishness, is it possible to be devilish with a young person who not only offers no encouragement, but who, in addition to the chaperonage of a brougham, is chaperoning herself with airs of profound contempt?

Reflections of this order are not propitious to enterprise. Only the unexpected is. Then, precisely as it always happens in life, and sometimes in fiction, the unexpected occurred. The Rue de la Boëtie — seductive and significant name! — had been reached, and through the torrent of traps which of a May afternoon pours that way, the girl was attempting to cross the avenue.

Midway on that avenue is a refuge. Before she could land there a tricycle swooped suddenly. It was within an inch of her. But athletics serve one in some stead. Before that inch could be covered Harry grabbed her, lifted her off her feet, pulled her bodily

back. She was in his arms, and he, with calm effront-
ery, was smiling in her face.

'Are you an heiress?' he asked. 'If so, you have
got to marry me. You nearly had us both run over.
After telling me to follow you, too ——'

'I told you nothing of the kind. I never spoke to
you in my life.'

Furiously she shook herself free, and angrily
looked about her. But in the torrent the brougham
must have been submerged. It was nowhere in sight.

'And now that you don't seem to be able to take
care of yourself,' Harry continued, 'and, what's
more, as you seem to have no one to do it for you,
I propose to take you home.'

'You will take yourself off,' the girl retorted, with
the same show of splendid anger. 'I never saw you
before. I never want to see you again.' And her eyes,
that were porcelain blue, flashed mightily.

'That's just it,' Harry dulcetly interjected. 'If you
were not so uncharitable you would help me. I am
a poor orphan, and I need assistance.'

'What you need is a policeman,' the girl threw
back. 'Now go find one, and let me alone.'

Caress a panther, and it will not necessarily rend
you. The girl had shown her teeth. They were royal.
But now from her voice the anger had gone. From
her eyes the flash had subsided. Harry noted the

change, and construed it properly. Château qui parle et femme qui écoute. From impudent he became resolute.

'Where are you stopping?' he asked.

At the question he stared deep into her eyes. She was fragrant as only a girl can be who has accounts all along the Rue de la Paix, and whose face is a wondering rose. As he stared at her she turned and looked much as the shipwrecked are rumored to do when in search of a sail. But in the seething maelstrom of the avenue, only tearing tilburys, scudding Stanhopes, and fleeting phaetons were discernible. The brougham was nowhere in sight, and helplessly she sighed and smiled.

'Across the way, at the Albe,' she answered at last, the point of her tongue just visible.

'Hurry, then, here's a chance.' And without further preliminaries, yet with two fingers on her elbow, Harry propelled her through a channel which a sergeant-de-ville had conveniently engineered.

'You know', he added, when ultimately the opposite shore was reached, 'that when they run you down here they fine you, too. That is the reason of my solicitude.'

'Then your solicitude may cease. This is my hotel. If you presume to follow me any further, there will be somebody to show you the door.'

'Why, I can see it from here, and a very fine door it is. Would you wish me to examine it more in detail?'

But at this he raised his hat. A cab had rattled up, and a gray-bearded Englishman, who had got from the cab, was addressing the girl.

'You are just in time,' she exclaimed. 'Lord Chudleigh, let me introduce a gentleman — whom I do not know.' And, with an expression that succeeded in being both diabolic and demure, she passed into the porte-cochére.

Harry's eyes accompanied her. Then, with a look of entire sweetness, he turned:

'Yes, there's the devil of it. I haven't the honor of knowing her, either. A locomotive was pouncing upon her a moment ago, and I took the liberty of saving her life. My name is Beamish,' he added, modestly.

'Hello! No relation to Josiah T.?'

'Unfortunately, his son.'

'Hello! Why unfortunately?'

'Oh, for a hundred reasons. I'll skip two or three. He wants me to marry. Wants, did I say? He is holding me up.'

'That's Josiah T. all over. He wants what he wants more than all others that want it, too. But, never mind. I'll have a talk with him. One good turn deserves another. Meanwhile, you might come in and give us all the facts in your melancholy case. My daughter must be expecting them. Yes?'

'Why, you are a brick,' Harry exclaimed. 'I had an idea, though, that your daughter was an American.'

'Yes? This way.'

Then, presently, Harry found himself au premier, in a canary-colored salon, staring again at the prettiest little girl in the world. She seemed but indifferently surprised to see him and but indifferently interested in the rather delayed introduction which ensued.

'Yes,' added Lord Chudleigh, when that ceremony had been effected. 'You might give him some tea. And some tears, too, Maud. Unless he marries somebody or other he will be cut off with a million. Yes. I'll be back directly.'

'He is a brick,' Harry announced, as the door closed. 'I just told him so. Now I may add that you are an angel.'

'And I may remark that you are very presuming.'

The girl was seated in a low chair. Her hat was gone, her gloves, too. She was playing with her fingers, the sunlight shuttling her hair, an image of Caprice retouched by Doucet. 'And so you are to be married, are you?'

'I hope I am,' Harry, with sudden rapture, replied.

'I would marry tomorrow if you would have me. Marry tomorrow!' he interrupted himself to exclaim: 'I would marry right now.'

'Nonsense, you are to do as you are told. Who is the lady?'

'An escaped lunatic.'

The girl nodded, with curious sympathy. 'You poor thing,' she murmured. 'No wonder I thought you needed protection. And you are such a dear,' she added, absently. 'I do think it a shame.'

Harry moved closer. 'Am I a dear?' he asked, in a little innocent voice. 'Tell me that I am.'

'You are a very enterprising young man, that's what you are,' she cried, releasing a hand he had caught. 'Can't you behave?'

But already Harry had retreated. From without there had come the sound of familiar voices, punctuated by an equally familiar wail.

'As I am a sinner,' he gasped; 'there's that tomcat!'

'Don't be ridiculous. It is only some relatives of mine. By the way, didn't I see you this afternoon helping them into a cab?'

Harry, unnerved, unmanned, undone, was too abject for reply. The door had opened, and before him a horrible trio; the duchess, her daughter, and his father, stood.

'Hello!' and through a lateral entrance a bearded face emerged.

'Yes, Chudleigh, it is I,' the duchess announced. 'The butler fell dead, and while he was being removed Angelica suggested coming here, and that, I think, showed such a sweet disposition.'

'Seraphic! But where did you pick up Beamish?'

'Oho,' said the fat man, 'I stopped in for tea at your sister's, and when the butler dropped dead, as the duke was at the dentist's ——'

'And if that isn't Mr Harry,' the duchess interrupted. 'Angelica, did you see Mr Harry?'

Harry, at the moment, was crossing the room.

'How did you get here?' Mr Beamish, in a hurried whisper, hoarsely inquired of him, and as hoarsely continued: 'Don't you know that — er —that little fascination of our friend is but a slight nervous affection, which only shows itself when she is excited, and which, anyway, matrimony will cure?'

'When who is excited?' Maud had surged, a hand extended. 'Mr Beamish, since every one has forgotten to introduce us, I am Miss Morningside.'

'We were talking, Miss Morningside,' the plutocrat answered, with a bow, which he executed as though it were a feat, 'we were talking of your charming connection, the Lady Angelica, and I was asking this young man if he knew that she had consented to

marry me. Yes, Me. We settled it just before the
butler ——'

But the sentence was never completed. Harry
exploded:

'Great Cæsar!' he cried. 'I don't wonder the poor
devil dropped dead. But isn't that too jolly?' he
added, turning to Maud. 'We shall be connections,
too.'

'What? What's all this about matrimony?' Lord
Chudleigh called out. 'I say, Beamish, you mustn't
ballyrag that boy into marrying any one of your
choosing. Give him his head.'

'Thank you, Lord Chudleigh,' Harry called back.
'But I wish you would give me your daughter
instead.'

'His stepdaughter,' the duchess severely corrected.
'Before her mother married my brother she had lost
her first husband, and that, I think, showed so much
savoir faire.'

Apparently, Lord Chudleigh did too. 'What?' he
exclaimed. 'Give you Maud?'

'He saved my life,' the young woman serenely
suggested.

'Hello! So he did! So he did! Pulled you out
from under a runaway baby carriage, I believe.
Beamish, what do you say?'

'What do I say?' answered the stock rigger, who,

with Wall street agility, had calculated to an eighth the value which this new vista of smartness unrolled, and who, in one swift, rapt vision beheld in his house a duke's daughter handing out grand pianos and polo ponies by way of cotillon favors, and an earl's step-daughter distributing diamond collars and four-in-hands. 'What do I say? Why, it rather strikes me that we'll corner the market; that we'll be top of the heap.'

'And that,' said the duchess, 'shows, I think ——'

Yet what it showed to the duchess no one seemed to heed. A maître d'hôtel, preceding a footman who was weighed down with tea things, had entered the salon, and was supervising their arrangement in a corner of the room.

During the progress of these solemnities Harry, who had been standing in the embrasure of a window with the prettiest little girl in the world, edged over to his father again.

'Did I understand you to say that that little fascination of the Lady Angelica only manifests itself when she is excited?'

'Well, what of it?'

'Miss Morningside and I have been talking it over, and we have decided on a wedding present for her, which, we think, may be of use.'

Mr Beamish sniffed with sudden suspicion. 'You

are getting devilish thoughtful of others. What is it?'

'A nice little cage!'

'And it is thoughtful of us, isn't it?' Harry re-marked, as a trifle overhurriedly, perhaps, he re-turned to where Miss Morningside stood.

'Yes, indeed; but let us think of ourselves,' that young woman answered, whereupon her hand was openly squeezed.

'Hello!' cried Lord Chudleigh.   'What's all this? Maud, come out of that window and pour the tea.'

'Yes,' said Mr Beamish, 'we don't want any more waiters falling dead. One is enough on a day like this. Isn't it?' he added, turning to Angelica.

And the duke's daughter, looking down at the carpet, blushed, as she answered: 'Meow.'

The Elixir of Love

The Elixir of Love

I AM married to a woman who is not my wife.'
It was on a liner, after dinner. The big ship
had lurched. Into the smoking-room where I
sat Lord Silverbridge had lurched with it. He had
dropped into a seat beside me. I had asked how he
did. It was in answer to that question that he made
this curious remark.

As he spoke he looked down and away and ran his
long, thin fingers through his bright, thick hair.

'What!' I exclaimed.

'And she is one of your compatriots, too.'

Lady Silverbridge — formerly Miss Fanny Bunker
— was a Bostonian. Of that I was perfectly aware.
At her wedding I had sent with my felicitations a
fish-knife. I had not been previously honored with
her acquaintance. But Silverbridge I had known
through a series of tolerably orgiac semesters at
Heidelberg, where his name was merely Jones.

Through what miracles of Death such processions
of relatives were mown that from nobody he had
become peer, it is idle to burden this narrative. Yet

the fact that we had worn identical student caps and fought identical student duels had eluded time; it had eluded, too, transitions and still survived. It was to this survival that I attributed the rather intimate confidence of his curious remark.

Of the purport of it I had not so much as an idea. The day previous I had embarked at Cherbourg for New York and found Silverbridge on board. It was then early in August. His marriage had taken place in London late in May. At the time I was on the Continent. It was the fish-knife that represented me. Subsequently the press supplied me with accounts of the wedding, of the bride's beauty as well. I never believe a word I read in the papers. But of the girl's beauty I knew by repute. In her picture I had seen that she embodied the ideal, filled the heart, and stirred it, too — just as Austin Dobson said of Autonoë — with pulse of Spring.

These things take long in the telling. But when Silverbridge made his curious remark, memory promptly ladled them out. I throw them in here to get rid of them.

'What!' I repeated.

Silverbridge looked up. 'Yes,' he presently resumed, 'it is beastly to boast, but I am up a bigger tree than any one you ever heard of. My wife is not my wife, and, though I am married to her, I am not her husband.'

At this, of course, possibilities of anterior entanglements suggested themselves. It occurred to me that when Silverbridge was Jones, he might, in some unhallowed moment, have gone and done it.

'You are not beating about the bush to tell me that there is another of them, are you?' I asked.

He turned to me quickly. 'How did you hit on it? Is it common — in the States, I mean?'

'Common! Common!' I murmured. 'I don't know that I should quite call it that. It seems to me devilish awkward. I haven't the Penal Code on the end of my fingers, but I fancy it must be ten years. How much do they give you in England?'

'For what?' he threw at me.

'Why, for bigamy,' I threw back.

He turned to me anew. 'I am not talking about bigamy.'

'Then what in thunder are you talking about?'

'Something worse.'

Smoke is a sedative. I hailed a steward, got a cigar, and proceeded to light it. Before the process was completed he was at me again.

'I have only one wife. That is to say, I have been married but once. But where my wife is I do not know.'

On the table before me was a passenger list. Already I had looked it over. Now I examined it once more. Among the S's was the following entry: 'Silverbridge, Graf und Gräfin mit Dienerschaft.'

'Isn't she on board?' I asked.

'No.'

'Then, without indiscretion,' I continued, handing him the list as I spoke, 'who is the lady mentioned here?'

At this he nodded to me, ran his fingers again through his hair, and made answer: 'There's the point. I do not know.'

'But,' I gasped, 'doesn't she know?'

'Yes, she knows.'

'Well, then, who does she say she is?'

'Miss Fanny Bunker.'

'But, confound it,' I cried, 'Miss Fanny Bunker is the girl you married.'

'Precisely,' he replied, and nodded again as though it ought now to be all perfectly clear. 'But then you see the Fanny Bunker whom I married and the Fanny Bunker who is on board are not the same.'

'Of course not,' I exclaimed. 'How could she be since she is now Lady Silverbridge. Previously she was a young girl. Now she is a married woman. That is difference enough.'

'The difference is wider than that,' he rejoined. 'Much wider. They are not the same person.'

I pitched my cigar away. 'Then will you please tell me how things got so damnably mixed?'

'Candidly, I can't.'

At that, in mounting irritation, I would have left him. It seemed to me that he was cracked. I was about to say as much. But something in the melancholy of his eyes prevented.

'No,' he added, 'I do not know how. But perhaps you can tell me. By the way, what was that stuff you used to stow at Heidelberg?'

'Psychology?'

'Yes, that's it. I thought of it when I saw you getting aboard. I thought, too, that because of it I might ask your advice. I am not boring you, am I?'

'Boring me! Give me the gist of this thing or you will drive me to drink.'

Silverbridge, however, was not to be hurried. He got a letter from his pocket, consulted it, consulted the ceiling, then, leaning forward, he made this extraordinary statement: 'There are two of her.'

I looked at him, but said nothing. After all, what was there to say? Yet, in my silence, there must have been the encouragement which he sought, for he ran on at once, quite volubly.

'It was in April we met. I cannot be sure, but I think between us it was love at first sight. I am sure, though, that I adored her at once. She exhaled all that is fetching in woman; simplicity, sympathy, sweetness, and strength. There was about her, too, an alertness, a vivacity, which I had never known. She went to my head. I think, too, I must have impressed her, for when I asked it was given. Our marriage was immediate. Somebody or other, a Frenchman I think, said that there are plenty of delightful marriages, but none that are delicious. The beggar was wrong. Ours was. But so appallingly brief! Four weeks, that is all. Yes, in four weeks she left me. One morning I awoke, aroused by a cry. At the other end of the room she was crouching and calling, "Where am I? Where am I?" And when I sprang up to go to her, she crouched yet further away, screaming, "Who are you? Who are you?"'

'The devil!' I muttered.

'You will understand in a moment what I did not. I assumed, of course — and it was horrible to assume it — that she had gone suddenly mad. But no, she was entirely rational, except in this, she denied any knowledge of or acquaintance with me. She denied that she was my wife. At first it was difficult to get her to believe even that she was in England. When

I convinced her of that she accepted the fact, but
not the marriage. She said she had had no part in it.
Meanwhile, it was obvious that she herself was
totally different. Her speech and manner had altered.
In no way was she the same. I got Simpson in.
Simpson you know is ——'

'Physician-in-ordinary,' I interjected.

'Yes, and he asked me concerning her antecedents.
I could tell him but little. She had come to London
for the season with some friends, and so soon after
I met her as I could manage it we were married by
special license. I told you it was love at first sight.
I told him so, too. He advised me to write to her
people.'

'Well?'

'I did. Here is a letter from her father. In it he
says that had he had the time, had our marriage not
been so precipitate, he would have told me — what
do you suppose? That within her are two souls. Is
such a thing possible?'

'Goethe said it was. "Within me," he declared,
"two souls reside." '

'But did they alternate? Her father says ——'

'That hers is a case of dual personality.'

'Yes, those are his very words. But is there such
a thing?'

'No,' I answered, after a moment. 'It is a term

serviceable merely for lack of a better one. You know, however, that the mind is dual. Ordinarily the two hemispheres of the brain work together. Now and again there is discord. The result is insanity. Less frequently while one of them is awake the other falls asleep, and vice versa. That, I suppose, is the case with Lady Silverbridge. What do you propose to do?'

'I have no choice. At her insistence and at her father's request I am taking her to Boston.'

'As Lady Silverbridge?'

'She won't admit that she is that. She declares that she is Miss Bunker.'

'Permit me. What is her attitude toward you?'

'H'm. Civil, but chilly. I think she hates me.'

'And you want my advice?'

To this question Silverbridge nodded hopelessly.

'Then,' I added, 'take her back as you took her from church.'

With the same hopeless look Silverbridge nodded again. 'Yes, it is easy to say, but nowadays there is no elixir of love.'

'Indeed there is,' I retorted. 'Given tact, opportunity, propinquity, and the desire and any man — who is a man — can change frigidity into affection; hate into love. But the ingredients must be fused. They constitute the elixir.'

To this Silverbridge assented. 'That's of course. But, for the elixir to work, the girl must be normal. Fanny isn't. She is abnormal.'

'I am not so sure,' I replied. 'And yet, if you come to that, are any of us normal? How often it happens that we do or say things that we had no intention of doing or saying, things which afterward we are unable to account for. In the course of every life there are such changes of personality that, could each phase of our existence be incarnated into distinct individuals and those individuals got together, so dissimilar and antipathetic would they be, that it is only a question of time when they would come to blows.

'No,' I presently resumed. 'We all change. It is a law of nature. But we change so gradually that the change is unperceived. Lady Silverbridge has changed, too, only the change in her instead of being gradual has been abrupt. But she is not, therefore, abnormal. For that matter nobody is. Every being, however constituted, has his or her raison d'être.'

'Yes,' said Silverbridge, after a moment. 'That is probably true. Yet, even so, I don't see how it helps me.'

'Why, very greatly,' I replied. 'The moment you recognize that the condition of your wife is normal you may proceed to administer the elixir. Your wife

is a young and sensitive woman. Barring a violin
there is nothing more impressionable than a woman
who is young and sensitive. Take, by the way, the
violin for analogy. In the hands of an artist it is
vibrant with harmony. In the hands of an artisan it
is discordant. Of course, there are violins so wretched
that no artist could draw from them quavers other
than cracked and thin. But, given a virtuoso and a
Cremona, and what duos, what trios even, the conjunction will produce! A young and sensitive woman
is a Cremona in flesh and blood. The harmonies, the
duos and trios of which she is capable depend on the
maestria of the man by whom she is approached.
Now you, I will assume, are a virtuoso and your wife
a violin. If you wish her to go with you to Boston as
she went with you from church, treat her as an artist
should.'

Silverbridge beckoned a steward and ordered beer.

'That is all very fine,' he remarked, when I stopped
to draw breath. 'Very fine in theory, but in
practice ——'

'In practice,' I interrupted, 'it is finer still. You
know the ingredients of the elixir. These ingredients
you have. You have but to compound them, feed her
with them, and once more she is yours.'

The steward approached with the beer. Silverbridge swallowed it, student fashion, at a gulp.

'Were not Lady Silverbridge already your wife,' I resumed, the process which I am about to indicate would be perhaps inconvenient, certainly unconventional, but not impractical. As it is, it will appeal to you as being entirely proper, poetic to boot, and psychologic as well.'

Silverbridge looked at his empty glass and then inquiringly at me. But, though there was an inquiry in his eye, the melancholy and hopelessness in them abided.

'Go to her stateroom tonight,' I continued. 'Go there when she is asleep. Go there when she is in her first sleep. Then whisper your name in her ear, whisper it again. Then again. Whisper to her that she loves you. But be careful not to awake her. In an hour return and whisper anew. Then leave her. The breathing of your name and the suggestion in her ear will make her dream of you, and in that dream it may be that the two hemispheres of her brain will begin to work in unison, or it may be that the one that knew you will be aroused and the other submerged. But in any event, whichever Fanny Bunker awakes tomorrow that Fanny Bunker will be yours. Then it will depend but on you to renew the harmonies you created.'

I stood up to go. For a moment yet he detained me. His face, previously drear, now was flushed.

From his eyes the melancholy and hopelessness were departing.

'Is — is this receipt one of your own manufacture or — or ——'

'You will not find it in the pharmacopœia,' I answered. 'But you will find it sovereign.'

'It has been tried?'

'Again and again.'

'Successfully?'

'Always.'

At this Silverbridge got also from his seat. 'Thank you,' he said very gravely. 'Thank you. I, too, will try it.'

With that for the night we parted. The next day I looked for him. He did not seem to be about. On the morrow, on the promenade deck, I ran into him. At his side was a beauty.

'Let me introduce you,' he said.

As he spoke, he smiled. The beauty smiled also. That smile of his and of hers supplied me with obvious deductions.

An exchange of the usual platitudes ensued. But the deductions I was in haste to examine. I made them into a bundle which presently, after more platitudes, I took with me to the smoking-room. There, later, Silverbridge joined me.

'The prescription worked all right, did it not?' I asked.

'Like an essence of bonbons,' he answered. 'I am married now to a woman who is my wife.'

'But to which of them?'

'To both,' he luxuriously replied.

'Lady Silverbridge is certainly a host in herself,' I ventured to remark. 'But then, so too is every Cremona. So is every impressionable woman. Should she get away again ——'

'If she should,' Silverbridge, with hopeful and beautiful confidence, exclaimed, 'if she should, have I not the psychologist's stone in this lovely elixir!'

'You have something better than that,' I concluded. 'You have love's writ of habeas corpus.'